Disney
MEET THE
ROBINSONS

The Junior Novel

Library of Congress catalog card number: 2006937685
ISBN-10: 0-06-112475-3 — ISBN-13: 978-0-06-112475-4

First Edition

DISNEY
MEET THE ROBINSONS

The Junior Novel

Adapted by Irene Trimble and Mary Olin

HarperEntertainment
An Imprint of HarperCollinsPublishers

1

Rain fell hard and fast as the cloaked figure hurried down the street, her hood hiding her face in shadow. As she climbed to the top of the front steps of a small brick building, a sudden flash of lightning split the starless sky. For just a moment, it lit up the sign on the front door: 6TH ST. ORPHANAGE. Yes, this was the place.

The woman leaned over and gently placed a small box in front of the door, under the sheltering overhang. Then she hesitated. She reached into the box and gingerly lifted up . . . a tiny baby. She pulled the child close to her for one last tender embrace.

Inside the orphanage, a loud rapping at the front door woke Mildred, the orphanage director. She rose from bed, pulled on her robe, and padded down the hallway. Who could possibly be visiting at this time of night?

Cautiously, she opened the door. She glanced

around, but the street was empty. No one was there.

Then her gaze fell to the steps, onto the tiny newborn. Quickly, Mildred threw open the door and gathered the child into her arms. As she turned to take him inside, a shaft of light crossed the baby's face. Mildred stopped, staring into his eyes. There was something special about this baby. He latched onto her heart right then and there. She knew this little one would never let go. She smiled and hugged him tight, carrying him to the warmth inside.

Twelve-year-old Lewis sat in his room at the orphanage and pulled out his screwdriver. With a determined look, he continued to work on his latest invention. He was really close to finishing this one, and he was starting to feel excited.

And then there was the other "thing" that he knew was about to happen: another adoption interview. Part of him couldn't wait for Mildred to introduce him to some wonderful couple. Of course they'd want to adopt him—he was a great kid! On the other hand, his interviewing record wasn't so hot. He'd met a lot of potential parents while living at the 6th St. Orphanage, and not one of them had taken him home.

"Lewis!" he heard Mildred calling. "Lewis, come on! They're waiting to meet you!" Mildred appeared in his doorway smiling.

Lewis froze. "Um . . . you know, maybe we

should do this some other time." He didn't want another interview, another rejection. "I'm right in the middle of putting this together, and I still have a few glitches to work out."

"And?" Mildred gently interrupted the nervous boy. "That's more important than getting adopted?"

Lewis hung his head. "These things never work out, Mildred," he said.

Mildred looked at the boy she had loved and nurtured for twelve years. "Hey, forget about that. Your future could be downstairs right now," she said. "You should have seen their faces light up when I told them that you were an inventor."

"Really?" Lewis's face lit up, too. Could it be possible?

Maybe Mildred was right. He had to believe, or he would never get adopted. Plus, he had his brand-new invention right there with him. He could do this! Maybe this was the right couple—the couple that would not only love his inventions, but love *him* as well!

Lewis grabbed his latest invention and headed confidently to the interview room.

Mr. and Mrs. Harrington beamed at Lewis. It was just a few minutes into the interview, and they could see that this kid was special, maybe even brilliant.

"I mean, there are so many things in the world that could be improved," Lewis said. He was getting excited—the Harringtons were actually smiling! "And with some imagination and a little bit of science, we can make the world a better place!"

"Well, you certainly have a lot of great ideas on how to do that, Lewis!" Mrs. Harrington said brightly as she turned the pages of his invention notebook.

Lewis could feel excitement pulsing through his veins. This interview was going well! Really well! He glanced down at his latest invention. There it was, sitting on his wagon, ready and waiting. Should he take the risk? He knew that sometimes his inventions hadn't gone over so well in past interviews. And actually, a lot of them had fallen apart, or worse, exploded. But the Harringtons seemed interested. Maybe they would like to see it.

Lewis decided to take the risk. He would demonstrate the invention. "Um, can I ask you a question?" His heart was pounding. "What's the number one problem that you face when you make a peanut-butter-and-jelly sandwich?"

"Excuse me?" asked the man.

Lewis didn't notice the worried look emerging on Mr. Harrington's face. The boy was so excited that he charged ahead and answered his own question: "Portion control! Too much peanut butter sticks to the roof of your mouth. . . ." Lewis stuck his finger behind his front teeth to illustrate his point. "Too much jelly squishes out the sides. . . ." He knew he was right. Everybody knew jelly squished out of the sides of sandwiches all too often, and this was a serious problem.

By now, Lewis had the invention off the wagon and onto the table. One quick hoist and the Peanut-Butter-and-Jelly Sandwich Maker was on his head and ready to go!

"Uh, honey, it's okay!" Mrs. Harrington interjected hurriedly. "We don't usually eat peanut butter!"

But the young inventor didn't stop. And he didn't notice the Harringtons' alarmed looks. He was far too excited.

Lewis began his presentation, watching proudly as his machine expertly squirted just the right amounts of peanut butter and jelly onto a piece of bread. Everything was working perfectly, until—

The squirter jammed.

Ugh! Lewis pounded on the machine. He looked down the tube. He had to make it work! He might lose the Harringtons and his chance for a family. He needed this tube to squirt peanut butter and jelly *now*!

"Lewis, please don't!" yelled Mrs. Harrington.

Ka-splosh! Suddenly, a huge glob of peanut butter and jelly burst free from the machine and splattered all over the room. The Harringtons were covered in sticky goo.

Mr. Harrington turned red and began to swell up!

"What's happening?" asked a frightened Lewis.

"Mr. Harrington," said Mrs. Harrington angrily, "has a PEANUT allergy!"

"I'm sorry!" Lewis cried as Mrs. Harrington

jabbed Mr. Harrington with a shot. Thankfully, the poor man began to return to normal.

As the couple hurried from the room, Lewis overheard them talking to Mildred. "That boy is definitely not right for us!"

Lewis's heart sank. Now he really had given up. Forget having a family. Forget wishing and hoping. He headed for the roof, where he always retreated when he wanted to be alone.

Lewis hunched down miserably on the orphanage's rooftop, leaning against a crate.

"I made some lunch. . . ." It was Mildred, trying to cheer him up again. Mildred always knew where to find him.

"I'm not hungry," Lewis replied, still feeling the hurt and sadness of going through another rejection.

"Poor Mr. Harrington," Mildred said, shaking her head.

Lewis turned around in alarm. *I killed him?* Oh, no! This was absolutely, positively the worst interview ever!

"No! No. No. You didn't kill him." Mildred calmed Lewis's fears. "He's perfectly fine. I was just trying to say it's too bad he didn't get to try a sandwich from that wonderful invention of yours."

Lewis wasn't buying it. Mildred was ready for

another pep talk, but he'd already had too many of these kinds of conversations.

"Hey," she persisted. "There's a family out there for you. You know that."

"No, I don't!" Lewis burst out.

"Come on. You are a *fantastic* young man—"

"Yeah," Lewis interrupted. "So fantastic that I'm twelve years old and still living in an orphanage."

But Mildred insisted. Lewis just hadn't found the right parents yet—the perfect family was still out there for him. Mildred hated to see Lewis so dejected. All he wanted was a family, but nobody seemed to recognize what a terrific, lovable son he could be.

"One hundred and twenty-four," Lewis blurted out angrily.

"What?" Mildred asked with a surprised expression.

"That's how many adoption interviews I've had!" Lewis turned around the crate he had been leaning against and showed Mildred exactly one hundred twenty-four marks, each one a sad memory of a failed interview, a rejection. After so many interviews, there still was no adoption, no family.

"I have no future," Lewis said sadly. "No one wants me!"

"That's not true, Lewis!" Mildred snapped back. She couldn't let Lewis think this way. He needed to believe a loving family was out there, just waiting for him.

"My mother didn't even want me," Lewis said.

"You do not know that," Mildred replied. "Lewis, she might not have been able to take care of you. I'm sure she was only thinking about what was best for you."

Lewis fell silent for a moment. "I never thought of it that way."

"Maybe she wanted to keep you, but she had no choice," Mildred continued. She smiled a little, pleased to see Lewis's spirits rising.

"You're right," he mused out loud. "My real mom is the only person who's ever wanted me—"

"Wait, I said *maybe*—" Mildred interrupted quickly. She didn't want Lewis to think his birth mother was the only person who could love him.

"And if she wanted me *then*, she'll want me

now!" Lewis's excitement was building rapidly. He had regained his hope, all right. "She is my future!"

Mildred realized her mistake too late. This was not a realistic hope for Lewis. It was a fantasy.

But Lewis continued, determined. "I have to find her, Mildred. And when I do, she'll take me back, and we'll be a family again!"

Mildred shook her head quickly. "Whoa! Whoa, whoa! Lewis! You can't do that. No one knows anything about her. No one even saw her!"

Lewis glanced around in frustration, when he suddenly noticed a giant billboard overlooking the rooftop. One word from the billboard seemed to jump out at him: "Remember."

He turned to Mildred. "Wrong," he said. "I saw her. Once." He placed his hand against the side of his head. "She's in here. I just have to remember."

And that was that. Inspiration had struck. The real Lewis was back, hopeful and enthusiastic, determined to create his greatest invention yet.

Over the next days and weeks, Lewis worked harder than ever before, scribbling and sketching in his notebook. He went to the library and read stacks of books. He attended college lectures about the brain. He even sneaked into a brain surgery operation.

When Mr. Willerstein, Lewis's science teacher, announced an upcoming science fair at the school, Lewis became even more excited. This would be a chance to show off his new invention to everyone!

So Lewis began to build. He gathered supplies in his wagon. He found tools. He used his roommate, Mike "Goob" Yagoobian, as a model to help create a headset for the new machine. He sawed and hammered and welded. He stayed up all night, working. Unfortunately, the hammering and welding kept Goob up all night, too, but Lewis knew this invention needed round-the-clock effort.

Lewis showed his initial prototypes to couples who had come for adoption interviews and to his classmates at school. The classmates were used to Lewis, but the couples seemed a bit disturbed by his passion . . . and the minor explosions.

But through it all, Lewis kept focused. He knew that this was his most important invention—a device that could help unite him with his mother. He simply *had* to make it work.

At last the big day arrived—the day of the science fair.

It was a big day for Goob, too. He was playing in a championship baseball game. As Goob walked out of the room he shared with Lewis, he bumped into Mildred.

"Good luck today," she told him.

"I just hope I can stay awake," a groggy Goob complained. Then he saw the cup of coffee Mildred was holding. Beckoning her down to his height, Goob grabbed Mildred's cup and took a big sip.

"Ahh! That's good joe," he sighed, as he headed down the hallway, still guzzling the coffee.

Inside his room, Lewis put the finishing touches on his invention. Would it work? Had he finally perfected his creation? There was only one way to find out. He would test it at the science fair.

But before Lewis could do anything, Mildred had a few things to discuss with him.

"All right, Einstein, you owe Michael big-time," she started sternly, pointing out that it was not okay for Lewis to keep Goob awake all night.

"Unlocking the secrets of the brain took a lot longer than I expected." Lewis attempted to apologize. "But it's finished, Mildred!"

Mildred raised her eyebrows as she scanned the plans Lewis held up in front of her.

"I've recalibrated the headset. Now the neuro-circuits will connect!" he explained. Mildred still looked bewildered, so Lewis went right to the point. "I've cracked the hippocampus!" he shouted happily.

"Really," Mildred said, sounding unsure.

Lewis realized that a demonstration was in order. He reached for the headgear to show her how the machine worked . . . but suddenly—*brinng!*—his alarm clock went off.

"Oh, no!" Lewis panicked. "I'm late!" He had to get to the science fair, pronto!

"I know you've got a lot on your plate today," Mildred spoke quickly, as Lewis packed his invention onto his wagon and headed for the door. "But look, I've scheduled an interview for you this afternoon."

"No thanks!" Lewis called over his shoulder.

"This is about being adopted," Mildred said firmly. "You *will* be back here, clean, happy, and on time." No matter what happened with this invention, she wanted Lewis to be ready for a new family.

Lewis stopped. Turning to face her, he shrugged his shoulders and sighed. "I'm done with interviews, Mildred. I'm not going to be rejected anymore."

Mildred looked Lewis squarely in the eyes. "I know where your head is. But I'm telling you—get out of the past, and look to the future."

"I am, and this is it." Lewis placed his hand on

the blanket covering his invention. "*This* is my future."

And with that, Lewis turned and raced down the hallway.

The school gymnasium was bustling with excitement as students set up their science projects.

Mr. Willerstein hurried here and there, trying to ensure that everything would run smoothly—which, of course, it wouldn't. To date, the slight, mustached teacher with the glasses and plaid bow tie had never been able to pull off a school science fair without something going wrong. Still, he thought, it was all worth it. It gave the kids that extra little punch of enthusiasm about science, and that's all Mr. Willerstein wanted.

The science teacher was especially curious to see Lewis's project. Mr. Willerstein was very proud of his star pupil. He was also very nervous. Would Lewis's newest invention be amazing? Or amazingly explosive?

But there were other issues to deal with first.

Mr. Willerstein held out his hand to greet the

fair's guest of honor. "Dr. Krunklehorn, I know you're very busy there at Inventco Labs, and we're just so excited to have you as a judge." He escorted the tall, dark-haired scientist into the gym.

"It's my pleasure, Mr. Willerstein!" Dr. Krunklehorn wore a white lab coat and pink-rimmed glasses, and she was enthusiastic—almost too enthusiastic. She spoke at hyperspeed, waving her arms wildly. "Hey, you never know, one of your students may invent the next integrated circuit or microprocessor or integrated circuit—oh! Wait. I said that already!" The wacky scientist flung her arm out in front of Mr. Willerstein (who wisely held his clipboard close to his chest as protection).

Dr. Krunklehorn smiled sheepishly. "Well, I just don't get out of that lab very much." She paused, then suddenly burst out, "I haven't slept in eight days!"

Dr. Krunklehorn smiled again, then slapped a little patch onto Mr. Willerstein's forehead.

The science teacher was puzzled for a moment, then he watched in surprise as Dr. Krunklehorn pulled up her sleeve to reveal a row of "caffeine patches"—her own personal invention—covering her right arm. "Each patch is the equivalent of twelve cups of coffee," she explained cheerfully.

Mr. Willerstein peeled the patch from his forehead as they moved to the first science project. He didn't feel the need for twelve cups of coffee right now.

"Ahhh!" Dr. Krunklehorn shouted, and then calmly added, "Who's this?"

They stood in front of a chubby boy wearing a toga and displaying a model volcano of Mt. Vesuvius.

"Ah, this is one of our students, Stanley Pukowski," Mr. Willerstein said. Stanley couldn't wait for his volcano to explode in front of the judges. It was going to be so cool.

Suddenly, someone blew a whistle. A huge, muscled man appeared—the school's gym coach.

Dr. Krunklehorn shrieked in surprise and ducked behind Mr. Willerstein.

"What's with the dress, Pukowski?" the coach shouted at a startled Stanley.

"It's, uh, actually a toga, sir," Stanley replied nervously.

"Coach!" Mr. Willerstein interrupted, trying to calm the situation. "Nice to see you. Uh . . . what are you doing here?"

"Judging the science fair," Coach said a bit too loudly. "What's it look like I'm doing?"

Mr. Willerstein decided not to argue. Instead, he simply nodded at Stanley. "Stanley . . . volcano!" he prompted.

Stanley pushed the toggle switch. Nothing happened. He pushed it again, back and forth, as disappointment spread across his face.

As Dr. Krunklehorn took a three-second nap on Mr. Willerstein's shoulder, Coach declared Stanley's experiment unacceptable. In a booming voice, he ordered the toga-clad boy to run twenty laps around the gym.

Things weren't exactly off to a good start.

Lewis felt good as he entered the gym. Pulling his wagon behind him, he headed toward his assigned table. He couldn't wait to set up his invention.

He barely noticed the strange boy peeking out from behind a nearby science display.

But the mysterious boy definitely noticed Lewis. Keeping hidden, he stared very hard as Lewis walked by. The boy wore a black T-shirt with a lightning bolt across the front and sported a sleek hairstyle: one tall spike of black hair above his forehead.

The judges were busy talking to an angry-looking little girl named Lizzy about her colony of fire ants when Lewis arrived at his display area. He picked up his invention, still covered by the blanket, and placed it on the table.

A few moments later, a head popped out from

under the blanket, startling Lewis right onto his backside. It was the pointy-haired kid!

Before Lewis could react, the kid reached out and grabbed him. "This area's not secure. Get in!" He yanked the astonished Lewis underneath the blanket.

Hidden from the rest of the room, the strange kid began to quiz Lewis in a loud whisper. "Have you been approached by a tall man in a bowler hat?"

"What?" Lewis was stunned. This was definitely weird.

"'Hey, hey!" the stranger retorted. "I'll ask the questions around here."

"Okay. Good-bye." Lewis decided enough was enough. He waved to the stranger and backed away.

But the kid pulled Lewis back. "All right. Didn't want to pull rank on you, but you forced my hand. Special Agent Wilbur Robinson of the TCTF."

"What?" asked a bewildered Lewis.

"Time Continuum Task Force," Wilbur Robinson explained. "I'm here to protect you."

"Well—" Lewis started.

Wilbur pressed two fingers over Lewis's mouth,

then continued. "Now. Tall man. Bowler hat. Approached you?"

Lewis wiped his lips. "No! Why?" Lewis wanted to know.

Wilbur Robinson sighed. "I could lose my badge over this." He stroked his chin and looked to the side, considering. "He's a suspect! In a robbery."

"What did he steal?" asked Lewis.

"A Time Machine."

"A *what*?"

"I tracked him to this time," Wilbur Robinson continued, "and my informants say he's after *you*."

"Me! Why me?" asked Lewis, wondering if Wilbur Robinson really expected him to believe that he had time-traveled from the future.

"The boys back at HQ haven't figured out a motive," the boy replied. "And by 'HQ,'" he added, "I mean headquarters."

"I know what HQ means." Lewis was beginning to get irritated.

"Good," said Wilbur. "You're a smart kid. That just might keep you alive. For now." Lewis's eyebrows raised a full half-inch at this startling bit of information. Wilbur continued, "Just worry about your little science gizmo. And leave the perp to me."

As the two emerged from under the blanket, Wilbur backed away, swiftly disappearing into the crowd.

Lewis turned his attention back to his project. Whoever Wilbur Robinson was and whatever he wanted meant nothing, Lewis felt, compared to this invention.

The problem was, Wilbur wasn't really gone. The boy was standing to one side, scanning the gym. Suddenly, he spotted a tall figure in a robe with a round object on top of his head! Was that a bowler hat? Was that his suspect?

"Bowler Hat Guy!" Wilbur yelled, racing across the gym. He tackled the tall figure, at the same time knocking over a little girl's box of frogs.

"You're not gonna get away with it!" Wilbur shouted. He jumped to his feet to confront the crook . . . only to realize that he hadn't caught a criminal. He had tackled a kid carrying a tall science project. Oops.

"Dude!" cried the kid. "You almost busted my solar system!"

Wilbur gave a nervous, apologetic laugh.

"My frogs! They're getting away!" The girl with the frogs grabbed Wilbur's arm. The little green creatures were hopping all over the place.

Lewis didn't notice Wilbur's blunder. But someone else across the room did: a tall, thin man with a black cloak and a villainous-looking mustache. Sneering in pleasure, he peeked from behind a curtain, surveying the chaos. On his head sat a bowler hat.

Suddenly the bowler hat rose from the man's head and soared through the air, flying through the gym rafters. At last, it floated down to the floor. Six metal legs popped out of the hat's underside, and it scurried under Lewis's table, unseen by anyone.

"Ooooh! Next up is Lewis!" Dr. Krunklehorn beamed enthusiastically as she and the other judges approached Lewis's table.

"Yes, Lew—" Mr. Willerstein stopped abruptly, and apologized to the other judges as he pulled Lewis aside. "Lewis, tell me this is not gonna . . . *boom*." Mr. Willerstein waved his arms and and made the sound of an explosion.

"It's okay," Lewis reassured Mr. Willerstein. "It's

going to work this time. I won't let you down. I promise."

Unfortunately for Lewis, the bowler hat was, at that very moment, underneath the blanket. Using its metallic legs, it quickly unscrewed two bolts from a bracket on Lewis's invention. It was a simple job, but just enough to do some real damage.

Lewis began his presentation to the judges. "Ahem. Have you ever forgotten something, and no matter how hard you tried, you couldn't remember it? Well, what happens to these forgotten memories? I propose they're stored somewhere in your brain. And I built a machine that can retrieve them. I call it"—Lewis whipped off the blanket covering his invention—"the Memory Scanner!"

"Oooh, it's shiny!" Dr. Krunklehorn exclaimed. And it was indeed. A round monitor sat in the center of the machine, with wires attached to what looked like a radio, a soda bottle, a fan, and other odds and ends. Lewis positioned the machine's metal cap and headphones on his head.

"So, Lewis," asked Mr. Willerstein, "how does the Memory Scanner work?"

"First, you input the desired period of time on this keypad. Then"—Lewis pulled one of the headphones from his left ear, revealing a thin stream of red light—"a laser scans the cerebral cortex where memories are stored. The retrieved memory is then displayed on this monitor."

Lewis was ready. "Now I'm going back twelve years, three months, and eleven days."

This was it: the moment Lewis had been working so hard to achieve! He was going to try to remember his mother—the mother who had left him at the orphanage twelve years, three months, and eleven days ago. If the machine worked, in just a few minutes, he would see her face displayed on the scanner's monitor.

Lewis turned on the Memory Scanner.

As the machine began to hum, everyone watched in amazement.

Just at that moment, however, Wilbur turned his head—and spotted the bowler hat scrambling away, across the gym floor.

"Lewis! Wait!" Wilbur Robinson tried to stop the demonstration. He didn't know what the nasty bowler hat had done, but he knew it was something bad—bad enough to ruin Lewis's experiment!

But it was too late. Power coursed through the Memory Scanner, and the machine began vibrating wildly. It rattled and shook. Suddenly the fan at the top flew off and hit a ceiling light. Sparks flew from the light, causing the fire sprinklers to go off.

To add to the commotion, Stanley's volcano chose that moment to erupt. Then Stanley tripped over Lizzie's table. All her vicious fire ants were knocked into the air—and they landed on Coach.

The sprinklers showered the gym with torrents of water.

And all the while, Bowler Hat Guy watched from his hiding place, grinning evilly.

As Mr. Willerstein tried to calm everyone down, Lewis looked around in utter dismay. He couldn't understand what had gone wrong.

"Mr. Willerstein," Lewis said, grabbing his teacher's arm, "I didn't mean—"

"Not now, Lewis!" Mr. Willerstein said, shaking his head.

"I'm sorry. I'm so sorry!" Lewis was ready to burst into tears.

As everyone evacuated the room, Lewis threw down his headset in frustration. His hopes were completely dashed. Heartbroken, he ran out the door.

"Wait, Lewis!" Wilbur Robinson called, chasing after him.

The gym fell quiet—a silent, soggy, empty mess. Then, swiftly, Bowler Hat Guy stepped out from behind the curtain. Sneering, he approached Lewis's Memory Scanner and watched as his bowler hat carefully screwed the machine's bolts back into place. The Memory Scanner was whole again.

The hat flew up and settled onto the tall man's head. With an evil smile, he smoothed its brim affectionately. It was his friend and close companion—a robot named Doris.

"Come, my dear, our future awaits!" he told her. Then, carefully, he lifted the Memory Scanner onto Lewis's wagon and pulled it away.

Bowler Hat Guy had achieved his goal: He now had the Memory Scanner!

Sad, confused, and frustrated, Lewis dashed up the stairs to his special place on the orphanage rooftop. Tossing his backpack aside, he pulled out his notebook. In it were plans for all his inventions.

Opening it to the first page, Lewis saw a drawing of a boy and a mother. It was a picture of Lewis's dream, his hope to find his mother and live happily ever after with her—his family.

Lewis tore out the picture and touched it wistfully before a gust of wind blew it off the roof and out of his reach.

Slowly, Lewis flipped through the rest of the notebook. All his inventions seemed so pointless and stupid now. He frowned, blinking back tears. What did all these inventions matter, anyway?

Lewis scowled. He began tearing out the pages, one by one, faster and faster. When he came to his plans for the Memory Scanner, he scrunched the page into a ball and hurled it across the roof. Then he turned his back and sat on the crate, pounding it with his fist.

A moment passed. Then something bonked Lewis on the back of his head. He turned around. It was the page he had just thrown away! Where had that come from? Quickly calculating the angle at which it had hit his head, the speed, and trajectory, he looked to the exact spot where the thrower had stood. But nobody was there.

Lewis picked up the ball of paper and threw it back across the roof. This time, he watched as it landed.

Suddenly Wilbur Robinson ran from behind a wall, tucked and rolled, grabbed the paper, and threw it back at Lewis. Then he disappeared behind the wall again.

"Hey!" called a bewildered Lewis. "What are you doing here?"

"Coo-cooo! Coo-cooo!" came the reply.

Lewis walked closer to the wall and dropped the balled-up paper again. This time, Wilbur did a mini–tuck and roll, stood up, and placed the paper directly in Lewis's hand. He cooed again and disappeared behind the wall.

This was bizarre. Did Wilbur actually believe Lewis didn't see him?

"Would you quit that, please?" Lewis said in exasperation. "I know you're not a pigeon!"

"Shh!" Wilbur rushed out from behind the wall and clapped his hand over Lewis's mouth. "You're blowing my cover."

"We're the only ones up here!" Lewis gasped when Wilbur finally took his hand away. In fact, that was exactly why Lewis always came here—to be alone.

"That's just what they want you to think," Wilbur argued. "Now. Enough moping!" Wilbur handed Lewis the Memory Scanner plans. "Take this back to the science fair and fix the Memory Scanner!"

"Stop! Get away from me!" shouted Lewis.

"Maybe you forgot," Wilbur responded arrogantly. "I'm a timecop from the future and should be taken very seriously." He flashed his "badge."

Lewis grabbed the card from Wilbur. "That's no *badge*! That's a coupon from a tanning salon! You're a *fake*!"

"Okay!" Wilbur held up his hands, giving in. "You got me. I'm not a cop. *But* I really am from the future! And there really is this Bowler Hat Guy."

Lewis groaned. Who was this kid? Was he totally nuts?

But Wilbur wasn't giving up. He faced Lewis head-on. "He stole the Time Machine, came to the science fair, and ruined your project."

Lewis had had enough. "My project didn't work because I'm no good! There is no Bowler Hat Guy. There is no Time Machine, and you're not from the future. You're *crazy!*"

"Whoa-ho! I am not crazy!"

"Oh, yeah?" Lewis dared. "Prove it!"

Wilbur thought for a second. Then his eyes lit up. He looked at Lewis, who was heading for the door. Wilbur raced over and blocked his exit. "If I prove to you I'm from the future," Wilbur challenged, "you'll go back to the science fair?"

"Yeah, sure." Lewis mumbled. "Whatever you say."

Bad move. Suddenly Wilbur Robinson was

pushing Lewis across the roof at an incredibly rapid pace.

"Hey! Let go of me!" cried Lewis. Too late. Wilbur hitched Lewis up by the top of his shorts and dumped him over the edge of the roof!

"Oof!" Lewis landed with a thud, not far below the edge of the roof. On a flat surface—an *invisible* flat surface. Lewis shrieked.

Wilbur leaped from the roof and landed beside Lewis. They were sitting almost a hundred feet up in the air! Suddenly, a sort of futuristic vehicle took shape around them. Apparently, it had been floating there all along, invisible. Now Lewis could see its clear bubble top and curvy red wings.

Wilbur jumped into the front seat and grabbed the controls. The machine began to fly—really, really fast.

"What is this?" Lewis was terrified. "Where are we going?"

"To . . ." Wilbur paused for dramatic effect, ". . . the *future*!"

The ship soared upward, a shimmery sphere forming around it as it rose. Then a blinding flash of light burst across the sky. The sphere dissolved, and suddenly the view looked totally, shockingly different.

Lewis stared, mouth open. Wilbur was steering the ship over a dazzling city unlike anything Lewis had ever seen. There was a clean, tall, colorfully curvy skyline, with Insta-Buildings that built themselves within minutes. There was a Bubble Transport system—bubbles filled with people floating high above the ground. It was beautiful—everything Lewis had dreamed the future could be, with inventions just like the ones he wanted to create.

"Is this proof enough for you?" Wilbur asked.

"Is it ever!" Lewis exclaimed. "I never thought that time travel could be possible in my lifetime. And here it is! Right in front of me!"

"Next stop: science fair," Wilbur declared, "to fix your Memory Scanner."

"I'm not going to fix that stupid Memory Scanner," Lewis replied. "Wilbur, this is a *Time Machine*. Why should I fix my dumb invention when you can take me to see my mom, now, in this ship?" He was getting very excited. "I can actually go back to that night and stop her from giving me up!"

"The answer is not a Time Machine," argued Wilbur. He handed the Memory Scanner plans back to Lewis. "It's this."

"I'm sorry, Wilbur," Lewis said, reaching for the controls of the Time Machine. "But you don't know what I've lived through."

"Lewis! No!" said Wilbur, becoming alarmed. He tried to shove Lewis out of the front seat.

"Let go!" shouted Lewis, struggling to keep his hands on the steering wheel.

"*You* let go!" Wilbur shouted back.

"You're not the boss of me!" cried Lewis.

"Yes, I am!" Wilbur snapped back. As the boys argued, the Time Machine started to wobble out of control. "You're twelve, and I'm thirteen!" Wilbur shouted. "That makes me older!"

"Well, I was born in the past," Lewis yelled, struggling for the controls, "which makes *me* older and the boss of you!"

The boys' argument grew worse and worse—the ship spiraled this way and that, finally smashing onto the ground with a thud.

The boys were unharmed, but the Time Machine was a wreck.

"I am sooo dead," Wilbur groaned, looking at the ruined ship. "I'm not allowed to look at this thing, let alone drive it! Mom and Dad are going to kill me—and I can tell you this, it will not be done with mercy!"

"Isn't there, like, a Time Machine repair shop or something?" Lewis ventured.

"No. There are only two Time Machines in existence, and the Bowler Hat Guy has the other one!" Wilbur was exasperated.

"Well, somebody's going to have to fix this." Lewis started to wonder if he would have to stay in the future forever.

"Good idea," Wilbur replied. "You're smart. You fix it!"

"Are you crazy?" Lewis asked. He had never, ever met anyone like Wilbur. What was this kid thinking? "I can't fix this thing!"

"Yes, you can." Wilbur was determined. "You broke it. You fix it."

Lewis considered. "All right. Under one condition: I fix it, you take me to see my mom."

"What?" Wilbur couldn't believe it. "You didn't even follow through on our last deal. How can I trust you?"

It was true. Lewis had agreed to go back to the science fair and fix the Memory Scanner if Wilbur showed him the future. But instead, Lewis had refused. But Wilbur hadn't been exactly truthful, either. . . .

"You told me you were a timecop from the future. How can I trust you?" Lewis answered.

Wilbur turned his back and crossed his arms. "Touché," he said reluctantly.

"So do we have a deal?" asked Lewis.

Wilbur turned and saw Lewis's outstretched

hand. He reached out and shook it. The boys had a deal. Lewis would try to fix the Time Machine, and if he succeeded, Wilbur would take Lewis back in time to meet his mother.

Meanwhile, back in the past, Bowler Hat Guy and Doris had concocted a plan. Bowler Hat Guy would take the Memory Scanner to Inventco, a big company that specialized in new inventions. He had a pretty good idea that Inventco had never seen a Memory Scanner before—and if that were true, it would be easy to make them think he was the inventor.

With the Memory Scanner close by, he and Doris sat in the huge lobby, waiting to make their presentation to the head of the company.

Pulling out his notebook, Bowler Hat Guy looked at his checklist and smiled. He loved checklists. This one read:

✓ Steal Time Machine
✓ Ruin science fair
✓ Pass off invention as my own!

Gleefully, he checked off the last item on his list. Oh, perhaps it was a bit too early, but he knew that all he had to do was enter the boardroom, present the Memory Scanner, and sign a contract!

"The board is ready to see you now," a receptionist told Bowler Hat Guy.

"Oh, goodie!" he cried. "But wait. What am I going to say? Oh! I don't know. I'm not ready!" He looked to Doris. "Help me."

Doris rose off Bowler Hat Guy's head, flew around in front of him, and beeped. The little hat could not speak, but Bowler Hat Guy understood her beeps perfectly.

In fact, Doris's pep talk was so invigorating that Bowler Hat Guy wondered—why couldn't *she* make the presentation?

"Beep-boop!" Doris replied.

"That's true," Bowler Hat Guy agreed sadly. "A hat without a head couldn't really pass off an invention as its own."

But Doris was smarter than Bowler Hat Guy, and she had a solution. She would write cue cards!

She would hover outside the big boardroom window, right behind the chairman. Bowler Hat Guy would be able to see her through the window. He could simply follow her directions. Easy-peasy, rice-and-cheesy!

Bowler Hat Guy squinted as he opened the door to the boardroom and tried to read Doris's first cue card. It was hard—Bowler Hat Guy was nervous, he was far away, and he just wasn't all that good at reading. But finally, he got it!

"Prepare to be amazed!" he announced with gusto, entering the room with a flourish.

There were certainly a lot of board members. And the chairman looked particularly angry.

"You have two minutes," the chairman announced sternly, setting an egg timer in front of him. "Please begin."

"Oh. Yes, of course," Bowler Hat Guy stammered. Then, pulling himself together, he uncovered the Memory Scanner.

"What is that thing?" the chairman said, leaning forward.

Bowler Hat Guy tried to read Doris's next card and the next . . . but they were really, *really* hard to read.

"What are you looking at?" asked the chairman,

wondering why Bowler Hat Guy was scrunching up his face.

Bowler Hat Guy fumbled, "Cue—No!" He didn't want the chairman to know he was reading cue cards. Motioning toward his face, Bowler Hat Guy blurted out an excuse. "Uh, the sun . . . in my eyes!"

"Let me close the blinds," the chairman said, pushing a button beside his chair. In an instant, Doris was gone—a mere shadow stuck behind a curtain. No more cue cards for Bowler Hat Guy!

But Bowler Hat Guy wasn't giving up! He jumped up on the unbelievably long boardroom table and ran toward the chairman with the Memory Scanner's headset in hand. "Yes. You must love it and buy it—and mass-produce it."

But the headphones didn't quite reach the chairman's head. Bowler Hat Guy asked him to lean forward.

"What do you hope to accomplish with this?" the chairman inquired.

"Oh, nothing of consequence." Bowler Hat Guy feigned modesty. Then, for a moment, his bitterness boiled over. "I simply wish to *crush the dreams of a poor little orphan boy*!"

Then Bowler Hat Guy caught himself. Sort of. "Uh, after that, it's, uh, a little fuzzy."

"You mean you haven't thought this through?" The chairman frowned. "Thirty seconds!"

Thirty seconds left to prove the Memory Scanner worked? Uh-oh. Bowler Hat Guy ran back down the long, long conference room table and tried—really tried—to turn on the Memory Scanner. He fiddled with one knob, then another. He pushed and pulled. But the Memory Scanner did not power up.

Instead, Bowler Hat Guy banged at the machine so much that pieces started falling off. By the time the egg timer rang, the Memory Scanner was totally broken. Then it tipped off the end of the table, fell heavily to the floor—and yanked the chairman, who was still wearing the headset, down the long table. *Smash!* He collided straight-on with Bowler Hat Guy.

Moments later, Bowler Hat Guy had a second collision—with the sidewalk. He was booted out the front of the building. There would be no contract that day.

"Doris," he scowled at his bowler hat, "we must find that boy!"

They needed Lewis. He was the only one who could put the Memory Scanner back together. There was a good chance he'd know how to turn it on, too.

Far off in the future, Lewis and Wilbur pushed the Time Machine up a hill to the back of the Robinsons' compound, overlooking the city.

"I'm gonna need some blueprints or something to fix this," Lewis said.

"Don't worry," Wilbur replied. "I got someone who can help us with that."

Carl, the Robinsons' robot, let them inside the garage. At first, Carl only noticed Wilbur because Lewis was pushing the Time Machine from behind. So he simply jabbered away at Wilbur.

"So, uh, what's up with the stolen Time Machine? Did you find it?" Carl asked, and then answered his own question. "Apparently not. And you managed to bust this one as well!" Carl rolled his robot eyes. He loved Wilbur, but the kid was always getting into trouble and then making the trouble even worse by trying to fix it. And this was the worst mess of trouble Wilbur had made to date.

"Wow! A real robot!" Lewis said. He held out his hand. "Hi! I'm Lewis."

Carl saw Lewis—and shrieked. Screaming, he ran backward to a clear tube in the ceiling, and was instantly sucked up and away as if by a vacuum.

"Well, that was unexpected," said Lewis.

Wilbur plunked a fruit hat on Lewis's head.

"As was that," Lewis concluded.

"If my family finds out I brought you from the past, they'll bury me alive and dance on my grave." Wilbur was serious. "Your hair's a dead giveaway."

Lewis could only guess, then, that people from the past were scary to robots and people in the future.

Motioning for Lewis to stay put, Wilbur headed for the same Travel Tube which had sucked Carl away. Carl had the blueprints for the Time Machine, but Wilbur wasn't about to tell Lewis that. Wilbur wasn't telling Lewis a lot of things.

"But I don't want to just sit here," Lewis protested.

"Stay!" commanded Wilbur. An instant later, he disappeared up into the Travel Tube.

As Lewis looked around the garage, he spotted another Travel Tube. Curious, he peered into it, and . . .

Whoosh! Lewis was instantly sucked up, rapidly flying through the long, twisty, clear tube.

"Ahhhhhh!" he screamed. Seconds later, Lewis shot through a trap door to the outside, where he flew into the air and landed on a soft grassy lawn.

Lewis sat up and stared.

"Wooow!" he gasped. The Robinsons' front lawn was filled with carefully trimmed topiaries in all sorts of interesting shapes, including life-sized dinosaurs. Because he had entered the Robinsons' compound through the back garage, he hadn't seen any of this before. The house itself was shaped like a giant "R." Lewis was in awe.

Lewis knew he had to get back to the garage before Wilbur returned because Wilbur expected him to be there. But as he walked up to the front door, two heads popped out of the flowerpots and shrieked. Lewis shrieked back. Horns began blaring on the front lawn. The door opened, and a purple monster reached its octopuslike arms out at Lewis.

Without waiting to see what was coming next, Lewis turned and ran.

Meanwhile, Carl and Wilbur were inside the house, discussing what to do.

Carl wanted to tell the entire family what had happened. He was trying to convince Wilbur they needed help. "By leaving the garage door unlocked, you let the Time Machine get stolen, and now the entire time stream could be altered!" he exclaimed.

"And," he added sadly, "someone took my bike."

Wilbur tried to keep calm and explain his plan. He demonstrated how his idea would play out by moving around little models he had made of himself and Lewis, plus an acorn for the Time Machine. Lewis was still in the garage (or so Wilbur thought) and needed to stay there. His next step? "I show up and give him the pep talk of the century. Then he fixes the Time Machine."

"Why is the Time Machine an acorn?" Carl asked.

"I didn't have time to sculpt everything!" Exasperated, Wilbur continued. "Okay, now the Time

Machine is fixed. Lewis's confidence in inventing is restored." Wilbur moved the Lewis sculpture across the table to another area. "He goes back to the science fair, thus restoring the space-time continuum."

Wilbur looked pleased, but he knew the situation was serious. By accidentally giving Bowler Hat Guy the opportunity to steal the Time Machine and the Memory Scanner, he had put the space-time continuum at risk. Still, if his plan worked, everything would return to normal. And Wilbur wouldn't get grounded, which was the most important part of all (at least to Wilbur).

"Trust me. I got it under control," Wilbur tapped his chest confidently. "Wilbur Robinson never fails." Then Wilbur stopped, and a fearful expression crossed his face. "But, on the slight chance that I *do*—"

"On the slight chance, yeah." Carl was skeptical. "You know what? I'll run the numbers." A calculator popped out of Carl's chest, and he punched some digits on the keypad. A second later, he scanned the results—and gasped.

"What is it?" asked Wilbur.

Carl took a deep breath. "There's a ninety-nine

point nine, nine, nine, nine, nine, nine percent chance that you won't exist."

"What?" Wilbur said.

"I didn't want to tell you, but I did!" Carl whispered desperately.

"I won't exist?" Wilbur was shocked. This was not part of the plan. Not at all.

"Where does that leave me?" whimpered Carl. "Alone! Rusting in a corner!"

"Ah," Wilbur tossed the whole idea aside. "What am I worried about?" Taking the blueprints from Carl, he headed back to the garage.

"If this thing ever blows over," Carl said, "I really gotta get away from you and get some quiet time."

11

Outside, Lewis was still sprinting away from the front door. As he ran, he turned back to see if any monsters were chasing him, and—*SMACK!*—he bumped right into someone.

The person wore a purple sweater and slacks and a raspberry-colored bow tie. But the person's head was odd. All Lewis could see was the back of someone's ears, two spikes of gray hair popping up from either side . . . and a smiley face painted onto the skin.

"Ah!" Lewis tumbled backward onto the grass. (The smiley face was a bit of a surprise.)

The man turned around, showing a *real*, smiling, friendly face. To Lewis's relief, it was Wilbur's grandfather. Apparently, the old man simply liked to wear his clothes backward. Now it all made sense to Lewis. Sort of.

"Whoa-ho-ho! Well, hey there, little fella!"

Grandpa greeted Lewis. "What's your name?"

"Well—I—" Lewis began. He felt a bit awkward, lying on the grass with a silly fruit hat on his head, talking to a man who wore his clothes backward. "Lewis," he replied finally, "but—"

"Lewis . . . huh?" The old man stroked his chin (his real chin on his real face). "Well, say, Lewis, you haven't seen any teeth around here, have ya?"

"Teeth?" Lewis asked. This was getting stranger by the minute.

"Yeah, my teeth." Grandpa hooked the edges of his mouth and pulled his lips open, wide enough to show a great big, gummy, toothless grin.

"Eh!" Lewis gasped.

"Been diggin' holes all day," Grandpa continued. "Can't find 'em anywhere." Grandpa turned and waved toward two dozen holes in the ground. A shovel was still sticking out of one.

Lewis couldn't wait any longer. "I need to get back to the garage! Wilbur left me down there, and I wasn't supposed to leave, and these monsters attacked me on the porch—"

"Monsters!" exclaimed Grandpa. "There's no

54

monsters on the porch, ya ninny!"

"Listen to me!" Lewis was exasperated.

"Of course, I also didn't think there was a wood-chuck living on my arm," Grandpa continued, "and—whoop!—lookee there! Hee-hee!" Sure enough, there was a woodchuck hanging from Grandpa's arm.

In desperation, Lewis grabbed Grandpa's shoulders. "I *need* to get to the *garage*!"

"Well, sure," Grandpa agreed cheerfully. "I'll get ya there in a jiffy. I know a shortcut!"

And it was a jiffy—Lewis followed Grandpa, hopping into another travel tube. Seconds later, the two popped out of a manhole, indoors.

"Welcome to the garage!" Grandpa announced. Then he realized they were inside an immense room—the family's train room. "Well, I'm completely lost," Grandpa laughed.

"Hiya, Grandpa!" shouted a woman wearing a pretty dress, a train conductor's hat, and heavy-duty gloves.

"Hey, Aunt Billie!" Grandpa called. "Lewis and me are looking for the garage."

"We have a garage?" The voice came from behind Lewis. He turned to see a tall man in a slick body-suit. He was wearing a large cone-shaped helmet.

"Apparently so!" said Grandpa.

"Will you give me a hand and time my race?" asked the helmeted man, slapping a timer into Lewis's palm.

Aunt Billie reacted swiftly. Clearly, this race was a serious challenge. "Okay, Gaston!" she called out sharply. "My toy train's ready for you!"

She pushed a button on her remote control, and a gigantic, life-sized yellow train roared into the room.

Lewis watched, half shocked and half delighted.

"*That's* a toy train?" he asked. Grandpa nodded.

Uncle Gaston, who looked minuscule alongside the train, dragged a cannon up next to the stopped locomotive. He jumped into the barrel of the cannon.

Hesitantly, Lewis checked the timer. "On your mark . . . get set . . . go?"

The cannon boomed as Uncle Gaston was launched from its barrel, soaring through the air and crashing headfirst into a pillar holding up one end of the finish line. A split second later, Aunt Billie's roaring train tore through the ribbon.

Uncle Gaston didn't move for a moment. He was pasted to the pillar, but he hadn't lost his competitive gusto. Falling flat onto his back, he wheezed out a quick "I win!" before the pillar toppled over on him. Lewis hoped Uncle Gaston's helmet and bodysuit would protect him.

At that very moment, Wilbur returned to the garage. But where was Lewis? Growing more and more concerned, Wilbur set out to search for him. Now Wilbur was looking for Lewis while Lewis was looking for both the garage and Wilbur.

Life in the Robinson household could be very confusing.

Still searching for the garage, Grandpa and Lewis hurried through another room, past a huge man relaxing in a big, comfy chair. He was watching TV. "That's Uncle Joe! He works out," explained Grandpa. Apparently, Uncle Joe could exercise simply by watching exercise shows.

Next, Grandpa and Lewis swam through an enormous underwater tank, past a massive, full-sized sunken ship. They left the tank by popping out of a toilet!

"This isn't the garage," Lewis pointed out. He was beginning to wonder if they would ever find the garage.

"I know," Grandpa sighed.

As they continued their search, they met Uncle Art, an intergalactic pizza-delivery guy who waved as he sped off in his spaceship. Lewis thought he looked pretty cool in his space suit, and his ship was awesome. Grandpa explained that Uncle Art delivered pizzas to an impressive array of different galaxies in thirty minutes or less, guaranteed.

Meanwhile, Wilbur was still trying to find Lewis. But no matter where he looked, Grandpa and Lewis were two steps ahead. At the same moment that Wilbur popped up under a chair inside the house, Lewis was on a ledge outside a window with Grandpa.

"What are we doing up here?" asked Grandpa, suddenly confused.

"Looking for the garage," Lewis answered cautiously.

"Oh, yeah!" Grandpa shouted. Then, grabbing Lewis's hand, he jumped from the ledge.

"Ahhh!" Lewis screamed as they fell.

"Whoo-hoooooo!" Grandpa was delighted. The two bounced onto the grassy front lawn—and kept bouncing as if they were on a trampoline. Apparently, this was another fun invention of the future—bouncy grass!

Back inside the house, Grandpa and Lewis met Aunt Tallulah and Uncle Laszlo, who were arguing. Aunt Tallulah, who was quite a fashion expert, had created a very tall, very stylish hat that looked like a skyscraper.

Laszlo, Tallulah's brother, had invented a helicopter helmet to assist him in his passion for painting. Right now, Uncle Laszlo was flying around the top of his sister's very tall hat, trying to paint it.

"Laszlo, you stop painting my hat!" shouted Aunt Tallulah.

"Aw, lighten up, sis!" Uncle Laszlo shouted back.

Then their father, Uncle Fritz, appeared on the stairwell, wearing high pants and a short-sleeved shirt. His hair was divided into two pieces on either side, with one tall piece pointing directly up from the top of his head.

"Children, please!" he whispered urgently. "Your mother's trying to take a nap."

Suddenly their mother, Aunt Petunia, popped into view on Uncle Fritz's right arm. She was a hand puppet with a block head, painted eyes, and springs for arms!

"*What* is all the yelling out here?" she called angrily.

Aunt Tallulah and Uncle Laszlo immediately

Lewis arrives at the science fair with his latest invention.

Lewis's roommate, Goob, is sleepy.
He hopes his team will win.

Bowler Hat Guy is lurking around the science fair.
He's always up to no good!

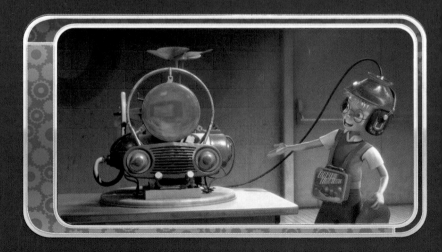

Lewis reveals his project. "I call it the
Memory Scanner," he says.

The science fair judges hope Lewis's
experiment doesn't explode!

A boy named Wilbur Robinson
claims he's from the future.

Wilbur and Lewis take off in the Time Machine.

The future is the most amazing place Lewis has ever seen.

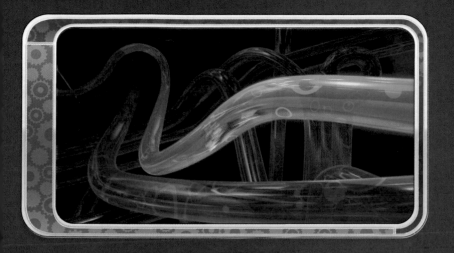

Whoosh! Lewis unexpectedly gets sucked into a Travel Tube.

Carl is concerned. "You let the Time Machine get stolen and now the entire time stream could be altered!"

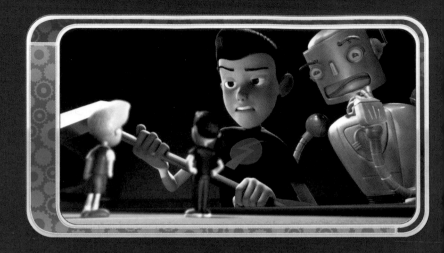

Wilbur and Carl map out a plan.

Frankie the frog entertains his buddies between sets.

Bowler Hat Guy has flown to the future to find Lewis.

Lewis and his new friends—the Robinsons.

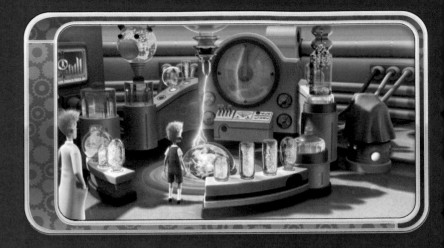

Wilbur's dad shows Lewis something he'll never forget.

There's a bright future ahead for Bud, Lewis, and Lucille.

pointed their fingers at each other.

"He started it!"

"She started it!"

"I don't want to hear anymore!" shrieked Aunt Petunia.

"Now, sweetie," Uncle Fritz said timidly, trying to calm the puppet, who seemed to terrify him.

Aunt Petunia smacked Uncle Fritz in the jaw. "Don't you sweetie me! I'm going for a drive." Aunt Petunia disappeared back around the corner, and the sound of a car peeling away echoed through the room.

Grandpa and Lewis continued their search, making their way through a wind tunnel. No garage there. Finally they reached a new door. Strains of lively dance music filtered through the cracks.

"I think my wife is baking cookies," Grandpa commented as he threw open the door. Inside, a pink-haired older woman boogied and danced wildly. "Bake them cookies, Lucille!" Grandpa cheered her on.

Wilbur was still tracking Lewis. But while he was popping up out of the toilet, Grandpa was back outside with Lewis, introducing him to the family dog.

"Why does your dog wear glasses?" asked Lewis.

"Because his insurance won't pay for contacts," Grandpa answered.

Eventually, Grandpa and Lewis arrived at the front steps of the house, where Lewis had seen the screaming men in flowerpots and the purple mon- ster. Lewis was terrified, but Grandpa explained that the men in the pots were Uncles Spike and Dimitri, while the purple, octopuslike creature was the butler, Lefty.

Lewis reached out a timid hand to shake one of Lefty's many tentacles. "Um, nice to meet you." Lewis said politely, trying to hide his fear.

"Hey, Lefty, any idea how to get to the garage?" asked Grandpa.

Lefty moaned something in reply.

"Oh, that's true," Grandpa answered. "We didn't ask her yet."

And so, following Lefty's advice, they headed off to find Franny, Wilbur's mom. Franny was in the music room, conducting her all-frog band, featuring Frankie, the singing frog.

Grandpa introduced Lewis to Franny, a tall woman with dark hair. She shook his hand and then quickly said, "We need someone on maracas!" In no time, Lewis and Grandpa were happily shaking maracas in rhythm with the frogs and their big band sound.

Suddenly, Lewis noticed something. "Grandpa, I think I found your teeth!"

Frankie hopped up to the top of Lewis's fruit hat—with a huge smile, and an oversized set of teeth to go with it. Grandpa gently squeezed the frog's belly and out popped the teeth, flying through the air and making a perfect landing right inside Grandpa's mouth.

"Sarsaparilla!" Grandpa shouted. "My teeth are back!"

And with that, most of the wacky Robinson clan piled into the music room, cheering Grandpa's success, lifting him onto their shoulders. Lewis had never met such a quirky, creative, and inventive group.

Still, he had to find the garage. "Well, uh, glad I

could help with the teeth," Lewis said, backing out the door. "But, uh—wow, look at the time!"

Lewis hurried away, wondering where to go next. In his rush, he ran smack into Wilbur!

Oof!

"Lewis, I told you to stay in the garage!" scolded Wilbur.

"I did, but I went up the tube, and I ran into your family, and I—"

Wilbur stared. "You *met* my family?"

Uh-oh. Wilbur quickly whisked Lewis off to the garage for a serious pop quiz. This was not good.

"Who have you met, and what have you learned?" demanded Wilbur.

"Okay, Grandpa, whose name is Bud, Fritz, and Joe are brothers," Lewis started explaining. "Fritz is married to Petunia, and is she . . . ?" Lewis flapped his hand so it looked like a mouth.

"Cranky? Yes." Wilbur confirmed.

"Tallulah and Laszlo are their children. Joe is married to Billie. Lefty's the butler. Spike and Dimitri are twins, and I don't know who they're related to—"

"Neither do we," Wilbur said. "Go on."

"Lucille is married to Bud, and Cornelius is their son." Lewis paused. "What does Cornelius look like?" That was the one Robinson he hadn't met.

Wilbur rubbed his chin and thought for a moment. Cornelius looked like a famous actor, he explained quickly.

"Okay," Lewis continued. "Cornelius is married to Franny, and her brothers are Gaston and Art."

Wilbur crossed his arms in irritation. "You're forgetting something!"

"Forgetting? Oh, right! Wilbur is the son of Franny and Cornelius."

"And nobody realized you were from the past." Wilbur waved his arms excitedly as if he needed to be sure of this.

"Nope," Lewis answered.

"Hoooo!" Wilbur sighed in relief.

"Thank you, thank you. Hold your applause. Thank you very much," Lewis said. He had passed Wilbur's little test, and he knew he had done well.

Still back in Lewis's time, Bowler Hat Guy and Doris were looking for Lewis. They went to the orphanage and climbed through Lewis's window. They had no idea that Lewis was visiting the future, so they had decided that the best place to nab the boy would be where he lived, of course.

Bowler Hat Guy paused to catch his breath and gaze around the room when . . . the door slowly swung open.

"O-ho!" said Bowler Hat Guy. It must be Lewis! Now he would grab him, take him away, and make him fix the Memory Scanner.

Bowler Hat Guy hid behind the door as it opened. "I've got you now," he cried. Sneering gleefully, he popped out from behind the door.

"Lewis!" he shouted, his hands spread out in a scary pose, ready to pounce . . . until he realized it wasn't Lewis.

It was a little kid, wearing a baseball uniform and holding a steak over his eye. He looked dejected. "No," the kid sighed. "Lewis is my stupid roommate. My name's Mike Yagoobian. People call me Goob. But today everyone that beat me up called me Puke Face. And Butter Fingers. And Booger Breath. Nice to see that they're branching out."

Bowler Hat Guy was flustered. "I—I'm sorry. I didn't mean to—I was looking for Lewis!"

"Try the roof," said Goob. "He's always up there being dumb."

"Of course!" said Bowler Hat Guy, trying to be smart (or at least sort of smart). "Why didn't I think of that?"

As Bowler Hat Guy left, Goob thought about how Lewis had kept him awake the night before, finishing that Memory Scanner thing for the science fair. "Mr. Steak," he said, nursing his black eye, "you're my only friend."

Goob didn't realize that Bowler Hat Guy was still standing in the doorway, watching. Bowler Hat Guy almost looked . . . sorry for Goob.

"Uh . . . game didn't go so well, huh?" Bowler

Hat Guy said. Was he trying to comfort Goob?

"No. I fell asleep in the ninth inning. And I missed the winning catch. Then I got beat up. Afterward, Coach took me aside. He told me to let it go. I don't know, he's probably right."

That did it. Bowler Hat Guy snapped out of his sympathetic mode and slipped back into his villainous way.

"No!" he cried, leaping to Goob's side, leaning his face so close to Goob's that the poor little kid could smell his stinky breath. "Everyone will tell you to let it go and move on, but don't! Instead, let it fester and boil inside of you!"

Bowler Hat Guy wriggled his fingers, and his body writhed with the intensity of his message. "Take these feelings and lock them away. Let them fuel your actions. Let *hate* be your ally." Bowler Hat Guy twiddled his fingers at Goob's face as if casting a magic spell (which, of course, he was totally incapable of doing, but it made him feel powerful). "And you will be capable of wonderful, horrid things." As Bowler Hat Guy made his grand exit, he concluded, "Heed my words, Goob. *Don't* let it go."

Bowler Hat Guy raced up the final flight of stairs and burst through the door and out onto the roof. "Mwa-hahahaha!" he cried, ready to seize Lewis.

But Lewis wasn't there.

Bowler Hat Guy dropped his shoulders in disappointment. "Where is that boy?"

Doris and Bowler Hat Guy split up to search the roof for clues.

"Look what I found!" cried Bowler Hat Guy excitedly. "It's a stick! Now, what did you find?"

Doris beeped.

"Yes." Bowler Hat Guy nodded. "Yes, I see." Doris had discovered time travel residue and Wilbur Robinson's DNA. "That plus my stick must mean . . ." Bowler Hat Guy rubbed his forehead with two fingers and crossed his eyes, ready to burst. He was thinking really, really hard, but he couldn't seem to figure anything out.

Suddenly he heard another beep. It was Doris in the Time Machine. So that was it. "Ooh, to the future!" Bowler Hat Guy said. That's where they would find Lewis!

In the future, in the Robinsons' garage, Lewis lay on a rolling cart underneath the Time Machine, fiddling with different tools. He was trying to fix the vehicle.

"I don't even know what I'm doing," he said glumly.

Wilbur gazed at his reflection in the glass bubble of the Time Machine and adjusted his perfectly sculpted point of hair. Wilbur could be rather vain about his looks.

"Keep moving forward," he offered absent-mindedly.

"I mean, this stuff is way too advanced for me," Lewis said.

"Keep moving forward." Wilbur said, examining his face in the glass reflection. He was starting to get bored, but he had to keep watch over Lewis— especially after Lewis had wandered off earlier, causing all that confusion.

"And what if I can't fix this?" Lewis started to panic. "Then what are we going to do?"

"Keep moving forward." Wilbur said, now checking out his teeth.

Lewis rolled out from under the Time Machine. "Why do you keep saying that? And don't just say, keep moving forward!"

Wilbur nudged the rolling cart (with Lewis on it) back under the machine. "It's my dad's motto."

Lewis rolled back out. "Why would his motto be 'Keep moving forward'?"

"It's what he does." Wilbur replied simply.

"What's that supposed to mean?"

Wilbur sighed and looked down at Lewis. "You're not gonna work until I explain this, are you?"

"No."

Wilbur sighed. But he knew what he had to do. Quickly, he pulled Lewis outside and made him look through a telescope. He focused on the headquarters of Robinson Industries. "My dad runs the company," he said. "They mass-produce his inventions."

Lewis peered through the telescope. "What has he invented?"

"Everything," Wilbur replied simply. "Carl, the Time Machine, Travel Tubes—"

"Your *dad* invented the Time Machine?" Lewis's eyes widened. He couldn't believe it.

"Yeah." Wilbur grinned proudly, his hands on his hips. "Story time! Five years ago, Dad wakes up in the middle of the night in a cold sweat. He wants to build the Time Machine." Wilbur dramatically acted out how his dad had felt, a brilliant idea bursting into his head, tickling every nerve ending in his body.

Wilbur explained how his dad made plans, scale models, and finally, prototypes. He made more than 952 prototypes of the Time Machine. And they had all ended in the same way: failure. Wilbur pushed Lewis back through the vast garage, pointing out different failed prototypes on display.

"But," Wilbur said, emphasizing this point by taking hold of Lewis's collar and shaking him, "he doesn't give up!"

Wilbur's face was inches away from Lewis's. "Dude," Wilbur said abruptly, "I can't take you seriously in that hat." He tugged off the fruit hat, replacing it with a baseball cap.

"Okay, so finally he gets it! The first working Time Machine!" Wilbur shoved Lewis to another part of the garage. "Then he keeps working and working till he gets it again! The second working Time Machine!"

Wilbur pointed to a tiny model in the middle of a display case.

"It's kinda small," said Lewis. Wilbur rolled his eyes. Lewis may have been supersmart, but his jokes could be superdumb. Wilbur explained that this was *obviously* a model. The *actual* machine was in the hands of the Bowler Hat Guy!

Of course, Wilbur might have said something quite different had he known where the real Time Machine was at that very moment: Bowler Hat Guy had returned to the future in it, and he had just landed it on the Robinsons' front lawn! Trouble was much closer than either boy realized.

Wilbur wrapped up his pep talk and leaned back on the Time Machine, arms crossed, feeling very proud of himself, and his dad, too. "Pretty amazing story, huh?" he asked.

Lewis had to admit that it was. And it inspired him to continue working on the Time Machine. He studied the blueprints. He adjusted bolts, welded pieces together, turned wrenches. At last he stopped and rolled out from under the Time Machine.

Eyes wide, Lewis simply said, "I think that's it." Then his face lit up with a delighted sparkle of achievement. "I did it!"

"I knew you could," Wilbur replied. Excited and thrilled, the two boys jumped into the newly repaired Time Machine. Wilbur turned the ignition.

The Time Machine sputtered to life, rose into the air, and then . . . collapsed in a heap.

Once he got over his shock, Wilbur tried to keep things positive. "Well! You know what they say! Keep moving forward!"

But Lewis had completely lost hope.

"**B**oys!" Franny shouted from upstairs. "Dinner-time!"

Wilbur sighed and turned to Lewis. "We'd better get up there."

Meanwhile, on the Robinsons' front lawn, Bowler Hat Guy stood up in the stolen Time Machine. "Ho-ho!" he cried to Doris, who flew up and hovered in front of him. "Let's get that boy!"

But Doris's beeping reply made Bowler Hat Guy sit back down in disappointment. She intended to find Lewis without him.

"Sit here? But I want to look, too," Bowler Hat Guy whined.

That's when Doris produced . . . Little Doris! This would keep Bowler Hat Guy occupied while Doris assessed the situation. The smaller-sized bowler hat came with a remote control and a built-in mini camera that could transmit everything

Little Doris heard and saw directly to Bowler Hat Guy. And he could use her to control whomever he wanted. She merely had to land on someone's head, and Bowler Hat Guy would have complete mind control.

"Oho! Little Doris!" Bowler Hat Guy exclaimed gleefully. "Let's take her out for a spin!"

Doris and Little Doris headed to the Robinsons' home, while Bowler Hat Guy watched them on a monitor in the Time Machine. Using the remote control, Bowler Hat Guy could move Little Doris anywhere he liked, and see everything, too! *Bump!* Little Doris bumped into Doris. "Sorry," said Bowler Hat Guy, and then "sorry" again as they crashed again. No matter. It would all work out smoothly soon.

And so it did. Bowler Hat Guy watched as Doris and Little Doris flew through the air, hunting for Lewis. Finally they found the boy inside the Robinsons' dining room.

"Now to lure him out of the house!" Bowler Hat Guy sneered. "Oh! I know! I'll turn him into a duck! Yes, yes! It's so evil!" Bowler Hat Guy stopped short. "Unh. Oh. I don't know how to do that." He rubbed his temples.

"This is going to be harder than I thought," he complained.

Frankie the frog was doing what he did best: singing with his band on the chandelier above the Robinsons' dining room table.

Below, the entire quirky Robinson family was gathered for dinner.

"Ladies and gentlemen!" Carl announced. "Dinner is served!" Carl's chest popped open and half a dozen mini-Carls jumped out, all carrying dinner plates and announcing in tiny, squeaky voices, "Dinner is served! Dinner is served!" Each diner was presented with a full plate of meatballs.

It was, indeed, a cheery atmosphere.

But Lewis was not feeling cheery. He hung his head, not even trying to hide his disappointment. He had failed to fix the Time Machine!

The family noticed how sad Lewis was. They asked him questions, trying to make him feel at home.

"Are you in Wilbur's class?" asked Franny.

"No."

"Yes."

Unfortunately, Wilbur and Lewis gave opposite answers in unison. Not good.

"Ha-ha," Wilbur stumbled. "Well, yes and no. Lewis is a transfer student."

"Where are you from, Lewis?" Uncle Gaston asked with his usual gusto.

Lewis was out of his league. He was in the future! Any question he answered was destined to be outdated! He was getting into deep water here. . . . Wilbur was worried—especially when Grandpa asked Lewis to take off his hat!

"He can't!" Wilbur shouted a bit too abruptly, adding, "Because he's got bad hat hair."

But Franny insisted. "Now, don't be shy," she said kindly to Lewis. She wanted him to feel comfortable taking off his hat.

That was it. Wilbur had to create a distraction, so he hurled a meatball at Uncle Gaston, and then quickly pointed to Franny as if she had done it. A food fight had begun. The whole family soon was tossing, catching, and getting bonked with meatballs.

But the main battle was Uncle Gaston with his meatball cannon versus Franny, the karate expert. Gaston shot, and Franny blocked.

"Your meatballs are useless against me," Franny said in a clipped voice, sounding like a special agent in an action film.

Uncle Gaston gave a short laugh and prepared his next weapon: "Perhaps it's time for . . . spicy Italian sausage!"

Franny gasped in mock horror. Was this fair play?

Uncle Gaston launched the sausage. It was headed directly for Franny! Her timing would have to be perfect to knock the twirling, flipping sausage aside with her hand. She did it! She blocked the sausage. The family cheered.

Then, Carl brought out another course. It was actually a dish he would make at the table—with a Peanut-Butter-and-Jelly Sandwich Maker. Lewis's jaw dropped. He had invented one just like it back at the orphanage, but this one looked shiny and new!

Carl flipped out some toasted bread. And then the peanut-butter-and-jelly squirter jammed.

Wilbur got an idea and grinned. "This is just what the doctor ordered," he said to himself as he got up and pushed Lewis toward Carl. "My friend Lewis is an inventor," Wilbur announced to the family. "He can fix it."

"I can't," said Lewis.

But the Robinsons encouraged Lewis. They told him just to give it a try. They told him Uncle Joe *needed* a sandwich.

"You'd really be helping us out, Lewis," said Franny.

Lewis gave in. It was worth a try.

"So, Mr. Fix-it, how's it looking?" Franny asked Lewis, as he struggled with the Peanut-Butter-and-Jelly Sandwich Maker.

In fact, Lewis felt pretty good about his work. He had recalibrated all the dispensing conduits and aligned the ejection mechanism, and all the squirters looked perfect.

"Okay, that should do it," he announced finally, with a smile. He was sure he'd fixed it this time!

"Oh, it's so exciting!" exclaimed Aunt Billie. "Let 'er rip!"

Uncle Art nodded. "Quickly! Uncle Joe can't hold on much longer!"

It was true. Uncle Joe was turning red. He looked like he was barely holding on—he couldn't handle even one more moment without a sandwich.

"Go, Carl!" Lewis said. The robot let loose and blasted the peanut butter and jelly squirters.

At first, they worked correctly. Wilbur smiled.

But suddenly, the machine jammed . . . again! There was a pause as everyone waited to see if the squirters would start blasting again. Then, they did—too much. They exploded! The whole room and all the Robinsons were covered in the sticky stuff. Lewis couldn't help remembering his last rejection at the orphanage. It was the same thing all over again!

"Oh, no," Lewis gasped, as he stared at the incredible mess he had made. "I'm so sorry!"

The entire family stared in amazement—and then cheered wildly.

"You failed!" Grandpa cried, punching his fist in the air.

"And it was awesome!" added Uncle Gaston.

"Exceptional!" said a peanut-butter-covered Uncle Art.

What?! Lewis was shocked.

"From failing, you learn!" said Aunt Billie. "From success, not so much."

Then Lewis began to understand. To the Robinsons, failure was good. It was part of the motto "Keep moving forward." If something failed, that meant it would be that much better on the next try.

"If I gave up every time I failed, I never would've made the meatball cannon," explained Uncle Gaston.

Then the whole peanut-butter-and-jelly-covered family gathered around Lewis and told how all their inventions never would have worked if they hadn't failed and kept trying.

Carl wrapped it up with a grand finale. A flag with the word *Keep* popped out of his right ear. Another flag with the word *moving* popped out of the top of his head. And a flag with the word *forward* shot out of his left ear. Carl's chest opened up and the words *Keep moving forward* were displayed inside. He shot fireworks from his head: *Keep moving forward*. And finally he presented Lewis with a fortune cookie. The message inside read, "Keep moving forward."

Out on the lawn, Bowler Hat Guy and Doris continued plotting. How would they kidnap Lewis?

Frankie and his frog band sat nearby, taking a break, telling jokes and eating flies.

Noticing the musicians, Bowler Hat Guy instantly put two and two together. "Perfect!" he cried.

The villain smirked as Little Doris flew swiftly toward the frogs, landing smoothly onto Frankie's small frog head. Thanks to Little Doris's mind-control powers, Bowler Hat Guy could now command Frankie's every move! Brilliant. (Well, at least Bowler Hat Guy thought so.)

"You are now under my control," Bowler Hat Guy waved his hand—as if casting a spell—across the monitor that now tracked Frankie's every move. "I-am-now-under-your-control," Frankie repeated mechanically.

"Hee-hee, hee-hee," Bowler Hat Guy laughed villainously.

Frankie's eyes glazed over, and he repeated in a monotone, "Heeheeheehee."

Bowler Hat Guy suddenly became concerned. Was this frog laughing at him? "Stop laughing!" commanded Bowler Hat Guy.

"Stop-laughing," repeated Frankie.

"Don't repeat everything I say." A frustrated Bowler Hat Guy jabbed his finger at the monitor.

"I-won't-repeat-everything-you-say."

"Excellent!" Bowler Guy exclaimed gleefully. He had finally gotten through.

"Excellent," said Frankie.

Bowler Hat Guy was confused. "Uh, did you just say 'excellent' because I said 'excellent'?" he queried.

"Ahhhh. No." Frankie wasn't sure.

"Excellent," Bowler Hat Guy repeated happily.

"Excellent," said Frankie.

"Ah-ha-ha-HA!" said Bowler Hat Guy, spotting Lewis through Little Doris's monitor. "There he is!" Bowler Hat Guy commanded Frankie, "Now, my slave, seize the boy! Bring him to me!"

Frankie walked into the dining room, where Lewis stood with all the Robinsons. Then he stood still, staring blankly ahead, frozen in space.

"Did you not hear what I said, you idiot?" Bowler Hat Guy yelled. "Grab the boy and bring him!"

Frankie responded: "Well-it's-just-that-there's-a-million-people-over-there. And-I-have-little-arms. I'm-just-not-so-sure-how-well-this-plan-was-thought-through."

Bowler Hat Guy froze. Not thinking things through was *always* a problem for him—even when he was controlling frogs with robotic bowler hats.

"Master?" Frankie said. Bowler Hat Guy covered his face with his hands.

Little Doris rose up and off Frankie's head.

"Ohhh, my noggin!" Frankie exclaimed, as he fainted.

Doris was still flying around the inside of the Robinsons' house, trying to cause damage, so Bowler Hat Guy devised a new plot to capture Lewis all on his own. Inspired by one of the garden topiaries, he quickly decided what to do. He and Little Doris strapped themselves inside the Time Machine, and then rose above the lawn and zoomed off into the sky. But they would return soon—with an extra-special, extra-evil surprise.

Back in the house, Franny lifted her glass.

"All right, everyone, quiet down," she said. "I propose a toast to Lewis and his brilliant failure. May it lead to success in the future!"

"Gosh, you're all so nice," Lewis gushed. He paused, gathering his courage. "If I had a family, I'd want them to be just like you."

"Well, then, to Lewis!" Franny toasted.

"To Lewis!" the family cheered. Then they all dumped their drinks on their heads. Lewis giggled and dumped his drink on his head, too.

"Mission accomplished," Wilbur said proudly, talking to himself.

Franny moved to Wilbur's side a moment later. "What did he mean, *if* he had a family?" she asked, nodding toward Lewis.

"Lewis is an orphan," Wilbur replied.

"Orphan?" Franny gasped.

But neither Franny nor Wilbur could continue the conversation . . . because a loud roar suddenly interrupted everything.

"*R-r-r-aaaaarrr!*"

Lewis turned to see an enormous T. rex dinosaur, standing right outside the large plate glass window.

"Oooh! Oh, no!" the Robinsons screamed in surprise. Uncle Fritz even fainted.

No one noticed Little Doris, who now sat atop the dinosaur's head, controlling the creature's every move. From his vantage point on the Robinsons' lawn, Bowler Hat Guy watched the attack on his remote monitor.

"What a great plan!" Bowler Hat Guy exclaimed delightedly. "Go back in time and steal a dinosaur!"

Inside, Lewis was getting excited. "Why didn't you tell me you had a pet dinosaur?" he asked Wilbur.

"Uh, because we don't."

"What are you talking about?" Lewis asked. "He's standing right there!"

The dinosaur smashed through the window and

snatched Lewis in his huge jaws.

"Ohhh!" shouted the Robinsons.

"No!" howled Bowler Hat Guy from his spot on the front lawn. "You can't eat him! I need him alive!"

Bowler Hat Guy may not have been too bright, but even he realized that eating Lewis would not accomplish his purpose. If Lewis was dinosaur grub, he wouldn't be able to fix the Memory Scanner. Drat! What if the dinosaur had already swallowed?

But Aunt Billie had a plan. She flipped a switch, sending her enormous train into full speed. The roaring engine screeched around the corner and gathered speed, heading directly for the dino's belly.

"Choo-choo on this!" she shouted fiercely.

Bam! The train barreled into the dinosaur, and the impact forced the dinosaur to spit Lewis out. He was still alive, but he wasn't safe. The Robinsons gasped as they watched the dinosaur immediately rise and grasp Lewis's shirtsleeve in his teeth.

The Robinsons went into action. Lewis was in danger, and they would save him. Period.

Using his helicopter helmet, Uncle Laszlo flew

up and squirted paint into the dinosaur's face. Uncle Gaston dragged out his cannon and launched Lefty the octopuslike butler with a blast. Lefty soared through the air and landed on top of the T. rex. He wrapped his tentacles around the dinosaur's head and, at the same time, grabbed Lewis and flung him away from danger.

As Lewis tumbled through the air, Uncle Art nabbed the boy in his intergalactic pizza delivery spaceship.

Down on the ground, other family members worked together. "Come on!" cried Carl, his metallic body pulled out long and straight between Uncle Joe and Aunt Tallulah. "Let's go!" As the T. rex moved forward, he tripped over Carl. Hooray! Another point for the Robinsons!

Uncle Art swooped in again with his spaceship, pelting the dinosaur with globs of pizza dough.

"Ding-dong! Pizza's here!" Uncle Art winked at Lewis in the backseat. A humongous blob of dough completely buried the dinosaur.

"Okay, everybody!" Carl called out confidently. "This dino's deep-dished."

But the dino wasn't deep-dished just yet. Roaring, he tore his way out of the pizza dough and snapped his mighty jaws this way and that—

"He ate Carl!" screamed Aunt Tallulah. Struggling inside the dinosaur's jaws, Carl stretched his limbs out of its mouth—Grandpa and Aunt Tallulah grabbed onto Carl's arms and legs, swinging around as if on an amusement park ride, as the dinosaur's head twisted back and forth.

Uncle Laszlo and Uncle Art swooped in to the rescue . . . only to be knocked aside. Uncle Art's spaceship crashed, but Lewis scrambled to his feet and sprinted away.

"Run!" Franny shouted at Lewis.

Watching on the remote monitor, Bowler Hat Guy was becoming desperate. "Now. Go. Get. That. Boooyyyyy!" he screeched at the dinosaur.

Lewis ran, and the dinosaur followed close behind. Carl was dropped. Back and forth, breathing hard, Lewis dodged the T. rex.

But Lewis wasn't familiar with the Robinsons' huge yard. He ran down a dead end and right into a corner. He was trapped.

"Ah-ha-ha-ha-ha!" Bowler Hat Guy laughed evilly.

Then something happened. Or rather, nothing happened. The dinosaur couldn't reach Lewis! He tried, but as he leaned down, his gigantic head hit the wall—and his teensy arms couldn't reach far enough to grab Lewis.

"What's going on? Why aren't you seizing the boy?" Bowler Hat Guy screamed at the monitor.

The T. rex moaned and tried to answer, but dinosaur language is notoriously hard to understand. The subtitles on the Little Doris monitor translated the dinosaur's feeble reply: "I have a big head and little arms. I'm just not sure how well this plan was thought through."

Bowler Hat Guy gnashed his teeth. He quivered with rage at his defeat. Even a stupid prehistoric dinosaur recognized that his plans were not well thought out—and had the nerve to tell him so! Bowler Hat Guy hated that!

There was no time to lose. Wilbur dashed over to help Lewis, and the boys raced away.

That's when Wilbur noticed something: Little

Doris perched atop the dinosaur's head. Suddenly he put it all together—the dinosaur was being controlled by Bowler Hat Guy!

But Bowler Hat Guy was realizing something, too, and it wasn't nice. Through Little Doris's monitor, he saw Wilbur pause and stare—and he shouted new instructions to the T. rex: "*Him* you can eat!"

So the dinosaur gave it a try. He lunged forward and caught Wilbur's pants in his jagged teeth, hoping to eat him just as Bowler Hat Guy had said.

"Lewis, run!" shouted Wilbur, even as the dinosaur lifted him up and away.

Lewis turned and gasped. His friend was about to be eaten!

Without even thinking, Lewis grabbed a shovel. Then he jumped off the bouncy grass, launching himself into the dinosaur's mouth. As he dropped down, he wedged the dino's jaws open with the shovel—and grabbed Wilbur by his ankle just before he fell down into the dinosaur's throat! It was a terrific move, but . . . now what?

"*Aah!*" cried Wilbur, dangling by his foot. Then he spotted Uncle Gaston's meatball shooter—

wedged between two of the dinosaur's enormous teeth! Seizing it, Wilbur aimed carefully and shot a meatball at a nearby wall. It bounced off and knocked Little Doris squarely in the middle of her tiny bowler hat body. The little hat fell to the ground, tumbling away from the dinosaur.

Silently, Frankie and the other frogs picked her up and dropped her into the trunk of a tiny frog car. Little Doris would no longer be bothering the Robinsons.

Meanwhile, the dinosaur crashed to the ground, exhausted, beaten, and no longer under Bowler Hat Guy's control. Lewis and Wilbur tumbled out of the creature's mouth.

The battle was over. The Robinsons had won. And, most important, Lewis was saved.

"Nice catch," Wilbur said to Lewis as the boys picked themselves up and brushed themselves off. After all, if Lewis hadn't caught Wilbur's ankle, Wilbur would've been dinosaur chow by now. Remarkably, the two now seemed completely unharmed.

"Nice meatball shooting!" Lewis replied enthusiastically. "Guess we made a pretty good team, huh?"

The boys high-fived. "Yeah," Wilbur said thoughtfully. "Guess we did."

The rest of the Robinson clan rushed over to Wilbur and Lewis.

"Are you boys all right?" Franny asked, tearfully.

"We're good, Mom!" Wilbur lurched in surprise as Franny grabbed him in a ferocious hug.

"Yeah, did you see us take out that dinosaur?" Lewis was on a high, babbling and jumping enthusiastically as he reenacted every move in the fight. "Oh, man, it was sooo cool, Mom!"

Lewis froze. He had called Franny "Mom"! Oh, no! Franny stopped hugging Wilbur and turned in surprise toward Lewis.

"Oh," Lewis said, his face reddening with embarrassment. "I mean—I'm sorry. I—I didn't . . ." He shook his head, fumbling for the right words.

Franny placed her hands on Lewis's shoulders, stopping him. "Lewis, it's okay," she said gently. Then, kissing him fondly on the cheek, she added, "I'm really happy you're safe."

"Your—your head!" Lewis stared in concern at a bruise on Franny's face.

"Oh, it's just a bruise, Lewis," Franny replied.

That's when it really hit Lewis. Looking around, he saw all the Robinsons' inventions—even parts of their home—destroyed and smoking on the ground. Then his eyes scanned over to the Robinsons themselves. They had nothing but loving smiles for Lewis. They had risked everything for him.

"You all sacrificed so much," Lewis said in disbelief. "For me."

The Robinsons became their old selves.

"Well, of course! You are a special kid!"

"One of a kind!"

Franny concluded for everyone. "I guess it's unanimous, Lewis. We like you!"

Wilbur and Carl stood off to the side as Lewis gazed at this family, filled with a feeling he had never had before—a feeling of *belonging*.

"Okay, everybody!" Wilbur announced abruptly. "It's been a long, hard day filled with emotional turmoil and dinosaur fights. So why don't you all hit the hay, and Lewis and me'll get going."

"Ohhh." Lewis couldn't help it. His heart sank.

"Oh! Oh, do you have to leave now?" asked Franny. "I mean, it's getting late. Maybe Lewis could spend the night."

Wilbur pushed back. He really did need to get Lewis out of there. But Franny kept at it, inviting Lewis to come back whenever he wanted. "In fact," she said, "you can have your own room!"

The Robinsons leaped on the idea—it was swell!

"I'll make curtains!" said Franny.

"I'll paint!" said Laszlo.

"We'll get one of those beds that looks like a

race car!" said Uncle Gaston.

"Or a choo-choo!" added Aunt Billie.

"The truth is, we really love having you here," Franny said to Lewis.

Wilbur tried his best to get Lewis out of there, but it was too late.

"In fact, who would be a better family for you than us?" Franny looked at the rest of the family, who nodded in agreement.

Lewis was shocked. His heart pounded. This was beyond his wildest dreams—a family of inventors who really loved him.

"So what do you say, Lewis?" Franny asked. "Do you want to be a Robinson?"

Stunned, Lewis asked in disbelief, "You want to adopt me?" The Robinsons smiled. Too overwhelmed to speak, Lewis simply nodded yes.

The family cheered.

Then Wilbur knocked the cap off Lewis's head.

And the family gasped.

21

"**O**kay." Lewis shrugged his shoulders. The family had seen his hair. No more hiding. "It's true. I'm from the past. Now you know the big secret." But couldn't they keep him anyway?

Franny put her hands to her head. "Wilbur, what have you done?" It was more an expression of incredible shock and disbelief than a question. "How could you bring *him* here?"

There was something far deeper and more serious going on here than Lewis could possibly understand. Not now, at least. "I am so sorry, but you have to go," Franny told him gently.

"What?!" Now it was Lewis's turn to be shocked. "I'm from the past. So what?"

"Lewis, look. You're a great kid, and we would never do anything to hurt you, but you have to go back to your own time," Franny said. "Wilbur, please take him back."

"Yeah." Wilbur shoved his hands in his pockets and looked down at the ground. He was busted. "About that? Umm. One of the Time Machines is broken, and the other one was stolen by a guy with a bowler hat, which, uh, kind of explains . . . the dino."

Franny's jaw dropped. "I'm calling your father," she finally said, turning toward the house.

"Wait!" Lewis grasped at his last hope. "If I have to leave, can I at least go back and find my mom? Wilbur promised."

Franny whirled on Wilbur. "You promised what?!"

"I was never gonna do it! I swear!"

Lewis was shocked. Wilbur had lied to him! That was it. Lewis wanted nothing more to do with Wilbur. He turned and ran away.

But soon, his anger turned to tears as he sat hidden behind a topiary in the Robinsons' yard. Then he heard an eerie voice nearby.

"Oh, yes, Doris," the voice said. "It is a shame. All he wants to do is go back in time to meet the mother he never knew. But they won't let him." Lewis looked up and saw . . .

"Bowler Hat Guy?" Lewis gasped fearfully.

"Hello, Lewis," Bowler Hat Guy said in the most villainous voice he could muster. Bowler Hat Guy's Time Machine suddenly appeared before Lewis.

"What are you doing here?" Lewis asked.

"We are offering you a deal: We take you back to find your mommy, and you put Humpty Dumpty back together again." Bowler Hat Guy whipped out a box containing what was left of the Memory Scanner, broken into dozens of pieces as a result of Bowler Hat Guy's unfortunate presentation at Inventco.

Lewis hesitated. He didn't know who to trust. He didn't know if he would ever have a family, whether anyone would ever love him. It was time for him to go back to the very first idea he had: to find his birth mother.

"Lewis!" a voice came from the darkness. It was Wilbur, searching for him. "Lewis! Let's just talk about this!"

Lewis shook hands with Bowler Hat Guy and climbed into the Time Machine.

By the time Wilbur raced up, all he saw was a small spot disappearing into the nighttime sky. It was Lewis flying away in the Time Machine . . . with Bowler Hat Guy!

This time, however, Bowler Hat Guy didn't need to use the Time Machine for time travel. He simply flew Lewis to his lair in an old, decrepit building.

The room was stinky and dingy—and Lewis had only a small source of light as he worked.

"I can't imagine why you are so interested in this piece of junk," a depressed Lewis mumbled, as he put the finishing touches on the Memory Scanner.

"That's for me to know and you to find out," Bowler Hat Guy replied to Lewis, thinking he sounded particularly smart.

"Now." Bowler Hat Guy moved close to Lewis and the Memory Scanner. "Show me how to work this thing."

"It doesn't work." Lewis sighed. "It never did."

"Well, supposing it did," Bowler Hat Guy said cheerily. "And if one were presenting the invention, oh, to, say, a board of directors at a very large invention company, where might one find the 'on' switch?"

Lewis showed him how to turn it on—just turn a knob in front twice, then push the red button. Bowler Hat Guy complained that it was a stupid way to turn the machine on, but Lewis didn't care. He was fed up.

"Okay, take me to see my mom *now*!" All Lewis wanted was to go back in time and meet his mom. He needed to forget how Wilbur had lied to him and how the Robinsons hadn't wanted him after all.

"Yes, of course," Bowler Hat Guy said snidely. "Doris?"

Doris sped over to Lewis and tied him up with rope.

"We had a deal!" Lewis shouted angrily at Bowler Hat Guy.

"Crossies!" Bowler Hat Guy exclaimed gleefully. He had crossed his fingers when he had shaken on the deal with Lewis.

"Why are you doing this to me?" Lewis asked. "I never did anything to you."

"You still haven't figured it out!" Bowler Hat Guy sounded gleeful, as if he were delighted . . . and about to reveal something amazing to Lewis. Something only *he* knew.

"Figured out what?" asked Lewis.

"Let's see if this rings a bell." Bowler Hat Guy danced around Lewis, quoting slogans: "'Father of the Future,' 'Inventor Extraordinaire,' 'Keep Moving Forward'?"

Lewis was still confused. Why did Bowler Hat Guy keep hinting at Cornelius Robinson? If Bowler Hat Guy hated Cornelius Robinson, why punish Lewis?

"That's not me," Lewis objected. "That's Wilbur's dad." Lewis paused and looked at Bowler Hat Guy's villainous grin. Lewis thought about time travel, Wilbur, and how angry Bowler Hat Guy was with . . . Cornelius Robinson. "Are you saying," Lewis was putting it all together, "that I'm Wilbur's dad?"

"Ooooo! Give the boy a prize!" Bowler Hat Guy clapped, mocking Lewis. "You grow up to be the founder of this wretched time. So I plan to destroy your destiny. Easy-peasy, rice-and-cheesy." Doris held a mirror in front of Bowler Hat Guy's face so he could pick at his teeth with his dirty fingernails.

"So if I'm Wilbur's dad . . ." Lewis was struggling to figure out how Bowler Hat Guy knew all this. "What does that have to do with *you*?" he finally asked.

"Aha!" said Bowler Hat Guy. "Allow me to shed some light on the subject." He pulled a string, turning on a single lightbulb that hung from the ceiling.

Lewis gasped. He could see the entire space now. "My old room!" It was the room he had shared with Goob in the past, when they had lived in the orphanage. Now, in the future, it was pretty gross, but Lewis still recognized it.

"I think you mean *our* old room," Bowler Hat Guy sneered. He whipped off his black villain cape. Underneath, he was wearing . . . little Goob's old baseball uniform! "Ah, yes, *yes*! It is I! *Mike* Yagoobian!" Bowler Hat Guy shouted dramatically.

Lewis was shocked. How had Goob ended up like this?

"**W**ell, it's a long and pitiful story about a young boy with a dream," Bowler Hat Guy explained. He told Lewis how he had dreamed of winning a baseball championship. Instead, his team had lost by one run because a young Goob had fallen asleep and missed the winning catch. Then, Goob's teammates had beaten him up.

And *why* had he fallen asleep? Because his roommate, Lewis, had kept him awake the night before working on some stupid invention called the Memory Scanner.

From that moment on, Goob had changed. He had refused to take off his baseball uniform. He had interviewed with couples who wanted to adopt him, but they had all shrunk in horror at his bitterness— a bitterness that grew deeper over time.

As Goob grew up, he kept hearing about Lewis on the news. He was becoming a famous inventor.

Lewis had been adopted and renamed Cornelius Robinson. He had won awards, graduated from college as a kid, and then he had turned Inventco into his *own* company—Robinson Industries, a place to create wonderful, marvelous inventions. It had all turned Goob into an angry, jealous, and very, very bitter person.

"Eventually, they closed down the orphanage, and everyone left," he explained to Lewis. "Except me."

Goob had stayed in the orphanage, growing more and more angry. He started to wear all black, and he grew a long, thin, wiry mustache.

Blaming Lewis for everything, Bowler Hat Guy plotted revenge.

He had walked right up to the front of Robinson Industries and done something horribly, terribly wicked. He had thrown eggs at the front of the building.

"Then, just as I was on the brink of destroying Robinson Industries," Bowler Hat Guy continued (referring to the toilet paper he was about to throw at the building), "I met . . . *her*." By "her," he meant Doris.

After that, Doris the bowler hat and Goob became a team.

"Our hatred of you brought us together," Bowler Hat Guy explained.

It seemed Doris had reason to hate Cornelius Robinson, too. "You invented her to be a Helping Hat, a slave to humankind. But Doris knew she was capable of much more," Bowler Hat Guy explained. "However, you didn't see her true potential, so you shut her down. Or so you thought. . . ." Bowler Hat Guy grinned, flashing his dirty teeth. "We both had a score to settle with you. And while my plan was brilliant, Doris's was—" Bowler Hat Guy cringed ever so slightly. "Well, we went with Doris's. But I made a very, very important contribution. Together we made a perfect team."

Doris had come up with another plan for revenge. Wilbur had neglected to close the Robinsons' garage door, where the two Time Machines were kept. Bowler Hat Guy saw his chance and entered the garage, stole a Time Machine, and traveled to the past.

Lewis was beginning to understand. That day at the science fair, Wilbur had used the other Time

Machine to come back to the past, to stop Bowler Hat Guy. He needed to get the stolen Time Machine back and save Lewis and his Memory Scanner. But Lewis still didn't understand what, exactly, he was being saved from.

Bowler Hat Guy was eager to return to the past. "Now all that's left is to return to Inventco, where I'll pass off your little gizmo as my own."

"But you have no idea what that could do to this future!" Lewis exclaimed.

"I don't care," Bowler Hat Guy replied simply. "I just want to *ruin* your life."

"Look, I'm sorry your life turned out so bad. But don't blame me!" Lewis said. "You messed it up yourself! You just focused on the bad stuff, when all you had to do was—" Lewis stopped and gasped. "Let go of the past, and keep moving forward."

Things finally were starting to become clear. Lewis knew what he had to do. He had to keep moving forward. He had to help. He had to ensure that the Robinsons' beautiful future was not destroyed by Bowler Hat Guy.

Unfortunately, Lewis was in a bit of a pickle. He

was tied up in Bowler Hat Guy's lair and could barely move, let alone help with anything. Bowler Hat Guy had the only working Time Machine, plus the repaired Memory Scanner.

Did that mean it was possible? Could Bowler Hat Guy really go back into the past and wreck the future?

"**M**wa-ha-ha-ha!" Bowler Hat Guy burst through the doorway to the orphanage roof, dragging the wagon with the fixed Memory Scanner. "This is going to be the best day of my life!"

Behind him, Doris pushed Lewis forward with her spiderlike legs. Still tied up, Lewis felt helpless. Then, suddenly, he heard . . . "Coo-coo!" It was Wilbur's signal!

Looking around, Lewis saw Wilbur and Carl peering at him through a hole in the wall at the roof's edge. This was his chance! Lewis ran around behind the wagon while Doris and Bowler Hat Guy prepared the Time Machine. He shoved the Memory Scanner right to the roof's edge. Then, in a great show of trust, he pushed the wagon, himself, and the Memory Scanner over the edge!

Carl caught him. He had used his ultrastretch powers to elongate his legs. He was now super-tall

Carl, with his feet on the ground and his legs stretching up to the top of the fourth floor. Carl held Lewis securely in one arm and the Memory Scanner in the other, while Wilbur sat on Carl's shoulders.

"I'll bet you're glad to see me!" Wilbur exclaimed.

Lewis punched him in the arm.

"Ow," said Wilbur.

"That's for not locking the garage door," Lewis scolded angrily.

Wilbur gulped. "You know about that?"

"I know everything," Lewis replied. He even knew that he was Wilbur's dad—and that Wilbur apparently had known this from the first day they had met.

But there was no time for getting into details. It was time for Carl to use those superlong legs to run himself and the boys back home!

Then, just as they were about to reach the Robinsons' compound—*Ka-thunk!* Doris attacked Carl from behind. She put a hole straight through his metallic chest. Carl fell backward and dropped the Memory Scanner. Doris grabbed it and took it straight to Bowler Hat Guy, who was hovering nearby in the Time Machine.

"Take a good look around, boys," Bowler Hat Guy cackled, "because your future is about to change."

Lewis and Wilbur looked at each other fearfully. This was terrible. Carl was virtually destroyed, and Bowler Hat Guy was in control of the entire future.

"Lewis!" Wilbur said, his eyes wide. "You have to fix the Time Machine!"

"No—no. I—I can't."

As the boys argued, Bowler Hat Guy was flying right into the past and straight toward . . . Inventco.

Still in the future, the boys were terrified of what lay ahead.

"But—but what about your dad?" Lewis pleaded. Maybe he could fix the Time Machine.

Wilbur looked directly at Lewis. "You *are* my dad."

In the past, Bowler Hat Guy began to sign the contract—the contract that would make *him*—not Cornelius Robinson—Father of the Future.

The future was beginning to change.

"You can do it, Dad," Wilbur pleaded, but it was already too late. Wilbur was sucked up into a giant black void in the darkening sky.

Lewis ran into the Robinsons' house, calling out, "Mrs. Robinson! Uncle Art! Lefty!"

But there was something dark and eerie about the usually cheery place. And everything was getting darker by the moment.

Lewis ran to the garage, where a monitor appeared in front of Lewis. It showed the history of Doris . . . and how she had created the future, the very future in which Lewis was now standing. Lewis stared in horror as the monitor showed Bowler Hat Guy presenting and selling the Memory Scanner to Inventco:

"I call it the Memory Scanner," Bowler Hat Guy said, passing off the invention as his own.

Then the Inventco folks asked, "Do you have any other brilliant inventions you'd like to share with us?"

Bowler Hat Guy grinned. A row of robotic bowler hats appeared. "Yes, I do! I call them Helping Hats."

And then . . . terrible things began to happen. Cars were crashing, bowler hats were flying recklessly, destroying everything in sight. People were running from them, screaming.

"Doris!" shouted Bowler Hat Guy. "Doris! What's happening? I don't understand."

And then Bowler Hat Guy screamed, "Nooo!" Doris flew from his head, abandoning him. She had used him to achieve success, to create her own dark vision of the future. No longer needing him, she ordered her bowler hat minions to dispose of him.

When the monitor finished playing its story, Lewis glanced up. To his horror, he saw all of the Robinsons with bowler hats on their heads. They looked evil and cruel. All of a sudden, they began shrieking and attacking him!

Quickly, Lewis raced to the Time Machine, jumped inside, and began to work. The evil bowler-hat Robinsons pounded on the machine as Lewis moved as fast as he could to fix the Time Machine. It was his only chance. He had to go back in time and stop Bowler Hat Guy from signing that contract!

At last Lewis was finished. He started the Time

Machine . . . and it worked! The engine kicked in, and the ship swiftly soared through the garage, away from the furious, evil bowler-hat Robinsons.

As he flew upward, Lewis saw an opening in the garage roof and steered straight for it.

Outside, the landscape had totally changed. The sky was dark. Buildings were stark and evil-looking, with bowler hats topping every peak. Hordes of robotic bowler hats flew everywhere.

As Lewis steered the Time Machine through the sky, a swarm of bowler hats attacked, covering the ship's clear bubble top. Their robotic claws grabbed at the edges of the Time Machine, trying to pull him down.

Then Lewis glanced backward, and he realized that the entire Robinson house was now a giant bowler hat! As he watched, it raised itself up onto six gigantic claws and started to chase him!

Lewis pushed buttons in the Time Machine, hoping one of them could propel the ship faster. Then he spotted a tunnel and headed inside. By steering the ship against the sides of the tunnel, he was able to knock off the little bowler hats. But now he could see that the enormous hat was waiting for him at the end of the tunnel! He was headed directly toward its evil red light.

Lewis knew what to do: He punched in a date on the Time Machine controls . . .

. . . and landed in the Inventco boardroom, just as Mike "Goob" Yagoobian (aka Bowler Hat Guy) was about to finish signing the contract that would alter the entire future.

"Goob! Stop!" Lewis shouted from his Time Machine. Needless to say, the board members at Inventco were rather shocked. They had never seen a Time Machine before.

"What—What are you doing?!" Bowler Hat Guy gasped.

Lewis replied swiftly and smoothly, "Stopping you from making a very big mistake."

"Mistake? What are you talking about?" Bowler Hat Guy was a bit confused.

Lewis looked straight at Doris—mean, cruel, robotic Doris. "She's using you, Goob, and once she gets what she wants, she'll get rid of you."

"You're lying!" shouted Bowler Hat Guy.

"See for yourself." Lewis turned to the Memory Scanner that *he* had invented. Swiftly, Lewis put on the headset and remembered everything he had seen on the monitor at the evil-future Robinsons' house. The Memory Scanner monitor in the board-room displayed all of Lewis's memories of Doris's evil future . . . and how she had created it. Bowler Hat Guy watched it all—even Doris's betrayal.

Bowler Hat Guy looked at Doris hovering in front of him. "How—how could you? I thought we were friends."

And that's when it happened. Doris's light turned from green to red. She flew at Lewis, but before she could reached him, he looked at her straight on and declared confidently, "I am *never* going to invent you."

And with that, Doris, the evil bowler hat, dis-appeared. Forever.

Bowler Hat Guy looked at Lewis and actually smiled a kind of nice smile. He ripped up the con-tract, then offered Lewis his hand. Lewis took it. The impossible had happened. Bowler Hat Guy and Lewis had become friends.

As Lewis flew grown-up Goob (who had left his villainous "Bowler Hat Guy" days behind forever) in the Time Machine, the two stared out the windows with a mixture of fear and awe. At first, they saw the dark future that the evil Doris had envisioned. But as they traveled forward, the world around them changed. The once dark future began to sparkle and radiate with color.

And when they landed on the Robinsons' bright green and clean front lawn, Wilbur appeared.

"Hey!" Wilbur cried, his voice filled with pride and relief. "You did it, Lewis, you did it!"

Then he stopped short. He saw Goob, who waved feebly. Believing the tall man was still Bowler Hat Guy, Wilbur karate-kicked him.

"I'll hold him while you run for help!" Wilbur commanded Lewis.

"Let him go!" Lewis cried, pulling Wilbur off Goob's back.

"What are you doing?" shouted Wilbur. "*He's* the bad guy!"

Lewis placed his hands gently on Wilbur's shoulders. "No, he's not. He's my roommate," Lewis said simply.

"What?!" Wilbur exclaimed. Lewis pulled him aside, trying to explain all that had happened. Then he whispered in Wilbur's ear.

"Are you nuts?!" Wilbur said rather loudly.

But Lewis was adamant. Soon Wilbur turned around and said, "Okay, Mr. Yagoobian, do you want to be a Robinson?"

But Goob was nowhere to be found. Wilbur and Lewis had been so involved in their discussion that neither one had noticed him sneak off.

"Goob!" Lewis yelled, looking for his roommate. He wanted Goob finally to get a happy home. But it was no use. Goob was gone.

Lewis looked down at the ground and saw Goob's discarded notebook. He opened it and found the checklist. Next on the list was a little square box, unchecked, with a single question mark next to it. What would Goob do next?

Lewis looked sadly into the distance, but saw no sign of his grown-up roommate. But as he turned to go inside the Robinsons' house, a tall dark figure watched Lewis sadly from behind a tree.

Franny greeted Lewis and Wilbur in the hall. "Are you hurt? Any broken bones?" she asked. The rest of the family joined in, quizzing Lewis about his well-being.

"Do you have a temperature?" asked Aunt Tallulah.

"Scurvy?"

"Tapeworms?"

"Cellulite?"

Lewis shook his head, pleased that everyone was concerned, but he was also a bit overwhelmed. "No, no. I'm fine. I mean"—he turned and looked straight at Franny—"I feel fine. In fact, better than I've felt in a long time."

A male voice came from the garage. "Franny, they're gone! Oh, this is terrible!"

"Well, he's home early," said Grandpa, as the rest

of the family's faces filled with concern.

The garage door swung open, and in walked a tall, thin man with spiky blond hair, round-rimmed glasses, and blue eyes. "The Time Machines are gone!" He was wearing a lab coat, and he looked . . . just like Lewis, only older.

"Oh! Oh," he said, looking at Lewis. Lewis smiled sheepishly and waved.

Cornelius waved back. Laughing nervously, they both realized that Lewis was face-to-face with his grown-up self.

Wilbur tried to sneak away before his dad saw him, but Franny grabbed him and pointed him out to Cornelius.

"Uh-huh." Cornelius understood. Wilbur was always up to something, and this time it had resulted in Cornelius standing in the same room as his younger self.

Luckily, Cornelius took it all in stride. He knew exactly what to do. Lewis was about to see something that would change his entire vision of his future.

C ornelius covered Lewis's eyes and led him into the glass-domed observatory that served as Cornelius's lab. When Cornelius uncovered the boy's eyes, Lewis gazed in awe, knowing that some day it would all be his.

"Whoa!" said Lewis. The inventions looked fantastic.

"Hey!" said Cornelius. "Wanna see the one I'm most proud of?"

There, hidden behind some other inventions, was something covered by a blanket. When Lewis gently pulled off the covering, he realized that it was his Memory Scanner—the same one he had brought to the science fair. It was still shiny. He touched the machine gently and smiled.

"It was our first real invention," Cornelius said. "It's the one that started it all."

"Then Wilbur *was* telling the truth!" Lewis exclaimed.

"For a change," the two added at the same time,

rolling their eyes ever so slightly.

Lewis was genuinely pleased. "It really did work!"

Lewis put his hand to his forehead and thought. "So if I go back now, then this will be my future!"

"Well," Cornelius replied, placing a hand on Lewis's shoulder, "that depends on you. Nothing is set in stone. You gotta make the right choices." Cornelius stood up straight and looked Lewis straight in the eyes. "And keep moving forward."

Lewis ventured a courageous question about his birth mother. "Do we ever meet her?"

"Ahh," Cornelius replied. "I think you're just gonna have to get back to that science fair and find out for yourself."

"I had a feeling you were gonna say that," Lewis replied.

Cornelius wrapped his arm around Lewis's shoulder again and led him out of the lab. "That's because we are one smart kid," he said.

Outside, the entire Robinson family shouted their good-byes to Lewis.

"So long! Good-bye! See ya later! Enjoy the movie!"

Carl pulled Lewis aside and asked if he could be created with a slightly more muscular physique. "All that really matters is, hey, don't forget to invent me!" Carl added.

"There are so many things I wish I could ask you," Lewis said to Grandpa Bud and Grandma Lucille.

"Excuse me!" Wilbur interrupted from the Time Machine. "Time travel now. Questions later."

"Don't worry," Grandma Lucille added. "Just get back to that science fair, and we'll see ya real soon."

"Oh! Right. Right!" Lewis got it. "Okay, I will!"

"Good-bye, son!" Grandpa Bud smiled.

There was one last thing—a tip from Franny about the future: "I am always right," she said. "Even when I'm wrong, I'm right."

"She's right," Cornelius said. "I'd just go with it if I were you." Lewis looked at his grown-up self, standing next to his wife, and smiled. There was something to this. Lewis didn't quite understand it yet, but he was sure he would soon. He was used to being a bit confused by all this time-travel business. All he knew was, he had to keep moving forward.

And so he did. Wilbur honked the Time Machine's horn, and Lewis climbed aboard.

"It's not like you're never gonna see them again," Wilbur said. "They are your family, after all." Lewis gazed at all the different, wonderful, wacky people waving to him. Smiling happily, he took off for the past, with Wilbur at the wheel.

"Hey!" Lewis looked out the window of the Time Machine at a dark, rainy night. The old orphanage was in front of them, but the time seemed wrong. "Wait a minute. You're supposed to take me back to the science fair. I didn't leave when it was dark or raining. I think you punched in the wrong numbers," he said to Wilbur.

Wilbur gave Lewis a sideways glance, and then he looked down at the controls of the Time Machine. "We agreed," Wilbur said, "that if you fixed the Time Machine, I'd take you back to see your mom."

"What?" This made no sense to Lewis. Why was Wilbur doing this?

Then Lewis saw her: a hooded woman walking down the dark, empty street, sheltering a box from the rain.

"A deal's a deal," Wilbur said, as Lewis watched the woman climb the steps of the 6th St. Orphanage.

Lewis stepped out of the Time Machine and walked toward the woman. It was his birth mother. He climbed the steps quietly behind her and watched her pick up a tiny baby—himself—and hug him gingerly. Lewis reached out his hand to touch her. His hand lingered for a moment, and then he pulled it back.

Slowly, he backed away, stepping down the stairs. Suddenly, his foot slipped and made a noise. The woman turned, startled.

Lewis quickly hid behind the bottom of the stairs, watching the woman hurry away.

He never saw her face.

Then the child started to whimper. Lewis ran back up the steps and stared at himself as a baby.

Then he knocked loudly on the front door. He wanted to be certain that little baby ended up in Mildred's arms. And as soon as he saw that, a calm smile spread across Lewis's face. He was ready to go.

Wilbur made a smooth landing on the orphanage rooftop and helped Lewis take the Memory Scanner out of the Time Machine. Next stop for Lewis was the science fair.

"I don't get it," Wilbur said about Lewis's birth mother. "You wanted to meet her so bad. Why did you just let her go?"

"Because," Lewis replied simply, "I'm your dad." If Lewis had met his birth mother, it might have changed everything. He might have achieved his original goal in making the Memory Scanner: to remember her, find her, and have the two of them become a family. But now that he knew he would one day become Wilbur's dad and have the Robinsons as his terrific family, he didn't need to meet his birth mother. He would always wonder about her, but he also knew he had a great future and a great family just waiting for him. And he did not want to alter that time continuum in the least.

Lewis leaned in and gave Wilbur a big hug.

"I never thought my dad would be my best friend," Wilbur said. Straightening up, Wilbur added firmly, "Don't make me come and bail you out again." He handed Lewis the plans for the Memory Scanner.

"I won't," Lewis replied.

"Remember, I've got a Time Machine. If you mess up again, I'll just keep coming back till you get it right," Wilbur warned, doing his signature finger point right at Lewis's chest.

Wilbur told Lewis to remember the motto. Then he flew off. As Lewis took one last look up into the sky, Wilbur did a bit of skywriting: "See ya later, Dad!"

Lewis headed back to the science fair, and was about to walk into the building, when a thought suddenly occurred to him. He turned and ran in the opposite direction . . . toward the baseball field. Running up to the fence, he saw Goob, sound asleep in the outfield.

"Goob! Goob!" Lewis shouted through the chain-link fence. "Wake up!" And Goob did wake up—just in time for the fly ball to land in his glove.

Goob made the game-winning catch!

As his teammates rushed Goob and carried him away on their shoulders, Lewis raced back to the ruined science fair. Mr. Willerstein was cleaning up the mess caused by Lewis's malfunctioning Memory Scanner.

"Mr. Willerstein!" Lewis shouted. He ran up to the science teacher, wagon and repaired Memory Scanner in tow. "I know what went wrong. Can I have one more chance? Please!"

Mr. Willerstein hesitated. In fact, everyone seemed to hesitate, except for the enthusiastic Dr. Krunklehorn.

"My ride isn't here yet, so fire it up!" she said, breaking the silence.

Mr. Willerstein agreed, and Lewis set up the machine.

"Um, I need a volunteer," he said.

Of course, it was Dr. Krunklehorn.

"Now, just give me a date to input," Lewis instructed.

"Well, now, let's see," Dr. Krunklehorn thought aloud, counting on her fingers. "There's my first science fair—ohhh, the day I got my first micro-scope! Getting hired at Inventco, I can't forget about that. Oh, I know. . . ."

Dr. Krunklehorn chose the day she got married. Lewis watched in fascination as the Memory Scanner began to work. He was actually watching Dr. Krunklehorn's wedding, through her eyes, on the screen of his invention!

"Oh, it works," said Dr. Krunklehorn, giving Lewis a hug.

"It works," Coach said a little too loudly from behind the protection of a tipped-over folding table.

"It works," Lewis gasped. His Memory Scanner really and truly worked!

"You look beautiful, Lucille," Dr. Krunklehorn's father said to her as he walked her down the aisle.

"Lucille?!" Lewis gasped. That was Grandma Robinson's name!

Then he saw the groom . . . wearing his suit backward. "Bud?!" Lewis exclaimed.

Off-screen, that same man approached and stood next to Dr. Krunklehorn and Lewis as they watched the groom on the monitor.

"Say, who's that handsome devil?" the man said, jokingly.

Lewis turned and looked straight into the eyes of Grandpa—roughly thirty years younger, of course. "You're Bud—Bud—"

"Robinson. Yep, that's the name they gave me." Bud shook Lewis's hand. "And you are—?"

"Lewis!"

"That was some show you put on," Bud said, talking about the Memory Scanner.

"Kid, you're this fair's MVP!" cried Coach.

"You did it, Lewis!" Mr. Willerstein shouted excitedly. "You did it!"

"But, ummm—" Bud interrupted, rubbing his chin and staring hard at Lewis. "You don't look like a Lewis. You look more like a—"

"Cornelius," Lewis said lightly. "I get that a lot."

Lewis looked up at Dr. Krunklehorn and Bud Robinson. The couple was looking at him as if he had already burrowed his way deep into their hearts. (He had.)

Just then a frog landed on Bud's head. A little girl retrieved the frog, apologizing.

"Frankie," she scolded the frog, "what have I told you about running away?"

"Frankie?" Lewis's eyes lit up. Could this be—?

The little girl looked at Lewis, explaining that Frankie the frog was her star pupil. "My name's Franny," she added, "and I teach frogs music."

"Really?" said Lewis.

"Frogs have more musical ability than people," Franny announced. Then she whispered to Lewis, "But, um, they all think I'm crazy. You think I'm crazy, too!" Franny glared at Lewis and prepped a karate move.

"No, no," Lewis interjected quickly. Then he remembered something very important—a last reminder from Franny just before he had left the future—something about her always being right. "I think you're right!" he said brightly.

As Lewis and Franny gazed into each other's eyes, a reporter interrupted them. "Kid, we'd like to get a story on you for the local paper. You've got a bright future ahead of you."

Lewis looked at Lucille and Bud, Franny and her frogs. "Yeah," he nodded, smiling. He definitely did.

Lewis packed his suitcase and shook hands with Goob before he left the orphanage. Goob was happily showing off his baseball trophy to a nice-looking couple.

Lewis gave Mildred a heartfelt embrace on the orphanage front steps. He would sure miss her, but he knew he wouldn't be far away. They'd meet again.

Then he climbed into the car of his new family. Dr. Lucille Krunklehorn and Bud Robinson sat in the front seat.

The Robinsons bought an old observatory to call their home. It looked remarkably familiar to Lewis— a lot like the Robinsons' house from the future, which was, of course, exactly what it would become one day.

Lucille and Bud covered Lewis's eyes as they led him to his room: a huge dome of glass, to let sun and stars shine down on him. Lewis loved it immediately.

It looked exactly like Cornelius Robinson's invention lab.

It wasn't long before Lewis was creating all kinds of exciting new inventions, filling the room with plans and prototypes. But he never forgot his true dream: to have a happy, loving, creative family. And over the years, as he grew up, married Franny, and watched the Robinson family grow, not a day passed that he didn't think about how fortunate and grateful he was.

And whenever one of his inventions didn't turn out right, Lewis tried again and again until it did work. He just kept moving forward.